Redemption in a New World

The New World Book Six

Sherry Derr-Wille

Published by Rogue Phoenix Press, LLP
Copyright © 2022

ISBN: 978-1-62420-706-8

Cover Art: Designs by Ms G
Editor: Amanda Armstrong

Dedication

To all of my family, friends and fans who have been waiting for this series to materialize.

Chapter One

Clint Anders rode slowly back to the ranch. The other hands left ahead of him, but he needed time to think. Try as he might, he couldn't remember how he came to be sent to Henderson Ranch. It didn't matter how he happened to be sent there. What mattered most was that he was sent there.

His first memory was of living in the dormitory with his friends, Parker, Roger and Jake. Together they'd learned how to be ranch hands and to live on the meager meals, if you could call them that, served by the Hendersons. At the age of six they'd been sent to work with the older boys on the ranch. Even so, they didn't know much about those who were older or younger than themselves.

His mind returned to the day Jake died. The day before, they'd been tending the cattle in the south pasture when they realized one of the prize steers was nowhere in sight. It was Jake who said he wanted to find the missing steer before he rode off, leaving Clint and the others to tend the herd.

Whether it was coincidence or planned, Henderson came out to where they were working. When he inquired about where Jake was, they told him about the missing steer and how Jake went out to find him. As soon as they finished telling Henderson about Jake, their friend reappeared leading the wayward steer by a rope.

"Where the hell have you been?" Henderson shouted as soon as Jake was in sight.

"There was a missing steer. I went out and found him. He…"

"It doesn't matter where he was. It's not your job to leave your duties. Come with me."

In his mind's eye, he could still see Henderson grabbing the reigns of Jake's horse and taking off at a fast gallop. Clint swallowed down the lump in his throat. That had been the last time he ever saw his friend alive.

The next evening when they returned from the range, Henderson brought Clint and his friends to 'the box' and told them to dig a grave for Jake. None of them dared to ask what happened. They knew that fifteen hours in 'the box' had killed their friend and life for any of them would never be the same again.

Three years later, he was horrified when he, along with his friends were sold to Senor Alfanso to be used as slave labor on his ranch. As the memory flashed in his mind, the brand on his upper left arm throbbed. It never bothered him unless he was remembering what his life was like before he was rescued and taken to the Alien Complex in Mexico City.

Their rescue and the Alien Complex had been like a dream come true. He'd been given a complete mental and physical examination in the hopes of finding any traces of his birth family. All throughout the search he held out hope, while enjoying the healthy meals and the education he'd been denied as a child.

He was surprised when Peter came to them in Mexico City and asked if they would be willing to return to Henderson Ranch, only now it was being called Resurrection Ranch. Clint knew Peter had been sold to Senior Alfanso but their paths hardly ever crossed. Like when they were growing up, they weren't encouraged to have communication with the men who worked in groups other than their own. Clint rode mostly with Roger and Parker as well as two of the older hands working on the ranch.

Shaking his head to rid himself of the memories he didn't want to relive, he thought about everything that happened to him since he arrived on Resurrection Ranch. At first, he was reluctant to return to the place that held so many horrors for him. The dormitory had been bulldozed and a new structure was in the process of being built. The only landmark he remembered was the main house. Even that looked different, boasting a fresh coat of paint, changing it from dingy grey to sparkling white with black shutters and trim. Somehow, he knew this was where he belonged. More than anything else he wanted to make a difference for, not only himself, but also for all of the others who had survived this hell hole.

The main buildings of the ranch came into view dissolving the memories of the past. Here was the future, only now he and his friends were down to two from four. Jake had been spared the horrors of becoming Alfanso's slave by dying in 'the box'. Roger had recently been killed by Jake's father as he looked for justice for his son in the worst way possible.

The healing period was beginning, at least that's what Jerilyn, the counselor on the ranch, kept telling them. He wanted to believe her but he was waiting for the next shoe to fall, so to say. Which one of the survivors would be the next to lose his life because of Henderson and the hell he'd put them through as children?

"Hey, Clint, what took you so long?" Parker asked, as Clint prepared to take care of his horse before washing up for the evening meal.

"I had some thinking to do. Needed to be alone for a while."

"If it was Roger you were thinking about, you have to put that behind you. I've been talking to Pastor Joel and he tells me the One God know the number of days we are allotted when we are born. I find that hard to believe, but it does make sense. If that wasn't the case, why would you and I have survived everything we did? I need to know more about the One God as well as all the other stuff we've been studying."

Clint nodded his approval of what Parker was saying. On the day Roger was murdered, he vowed to make Resurrection Ranch a memorial to Roger, Jake and all the other children who lost their lives at the hands of the Hendersons.

~ * ~

Josie Rawlins left Dr. Gratan's office, pleased with how well he thought she was healing. Physically, she had definitely healed from her father's beating, but mentally was another thing.

For as long as she could remember, her father told her how much he missed her brother, Jake, and he wanted to see justice done. How could she have ever known his idea of justice would be shooting an innocent man and wounding many others? To make matters worse, the man who had been killed turned out to be a good friend of her brother, Jake. Even though he was her father, she knew she could never forgive him. In trying to come to grips with it, she'd made an appointment with Pastor Joel to seek his help. Her appointment with him was scheduled for the next afternoon.

For now, she wanted to report to Hodia and tell her she'd been released by the doctor and was ready to begin helping out at the school. She prayed she would be able to work with some of the young men, since working with them would, perhaps, bring her closer to the younger brother she hadn't known.

Thinking of Jake brought Zander to mind. He had been used as his father's pawn to bring disaster down upon Resurrection Ranch and the young men who were working to make this ranch one of the most prosperous in the county. It still amazed her how willing they were to give Zander a second chance.

Last week, he'd been released from the hospital, and immediately began working with Mark Alamor, making certain the insurance coverage for the ranch was up to date. Although she knew Zander was one of the top insurance agents in the state of Iowa, she was amazed that the young men on this ranch were so trusting of him.

"You look like you have the weight of the world on your shoulders, Sis?" she heard Zander say from behind of her.

"Not really. I've been thinking about how quickly things change. One day we were living in Maquoketa, Iowa and the next we're associated with Resurrection Ranch. To make matters worse, Dad is awaiting trial for murder and attempted murder. None of it makes sense and yet, it's like this is where we belong."

"I know what you mean. I was a blind fool to follow Dad's road to destruction. To be truthful, I never expected forgiveness from the people here. Mark and I have been working together and I'm pleased to say we have formed a friendship of sorts. I'm still not certain if insurance is something I want to do for the rest of my life. I told him I might like to look into the architectural program his Uncle David is initiating. Do you think I'm too old to make such a change?"

"No one is too old to change. Look at Mom, she's back in Iowa closing out everything there and getting ready to move here permanently."

"What do you think she'll do here?"

"Before she left, she was talking to Connor and Julie, the chefs for this place. They're willing to train her to help them out and take over the cooking when they need time off. She's thrilled with the offer."

"That's good. Once I came to my senses and realized all the hate we grew up with was wrong, I worried how she would adapt to life without Dad."

"I'm certain you didn't know it, but she was considering divorce. He's been abusive to her for years. I saw it, even if you didn't. It was especially bad when she took the job at the restaurant. The night he snapped, he hurt both of us very badly. We can all be thankful for the advanced medical treatment we received after it happened."

"Don't I know it. You would hardly know that I was ever burned. I thought for certain I would be scarred for life. I have a lot of things to be thankful for."

"I hate to cut this short," Josie said, "but I have an appointment with Hodia to see when I can begin working at the school. This is the opportunity of a lifetime for me. I'm hoping to work with the older students, as Diane and Melian have the younger ones covered."

Zander gave her a brotherly hug before they parted company. He'd given her a lot to think about. She couldn't see him doing anything other than work in the insurance industry, but she admired him for considering doing something other than what their father told him he had to do.

She arrived at Hodia's office ten minutes early but she didn't mind the wait. She enjoyed being in the school building, daydreaming about being able to help teach the classes the older students would be taking.

"Josie, I'm sorry you had to wait," Hodia greeted her.

"It wasn't a long wait and I thoroughly enjoyed having the time to daydream about the future. I just left Dr. Gratan and he cleared me to begin work. I must say I'm looking forward to joining you."

"I'm pleased to hear you say that. As I told you earlier, we are shorthanded, especially where the older students are concerned. It's thrilling to teach the young children but a challenge to do the same with adults. You must realize some of your students would be your same age."

"I do. I've always wanted to teach adults. I was looking into teaching at our local vocational school, but there were no positions open.

If I was back in Iowa, I would be working as a substitute teacher rather than anything full time. I'm looking forward to this challenge."

"That's exactly what I wanted to hear. If you can start this afternoon, you can monitor the class that Diane teaches in the evening as well as the one in the early morning. When she thinks you'll be comfortable on your own, she will be happy to have more time to relax. Along with the classes for the adults, she's got a full schedule teaching with the younger children. Since that's where her expertise is, I'm sure she will be thrilled to be able to concentrate on their classes."

Josie left the office with the schedule for the early morning and late afternoon classes in her hand. After checking the time on her communicator, she realized it was time to go over to the dining hall for the midday meal.

~ * ~

Josie had little trouble in finding Diane's classroom. Rather than the smaller desks she'd seen in the classroom she toured when she first applied to work with the teachers here, the room was equipped with tables and chairs that would accommodate the older students. There were three tables with the chairs to go with them reminding her that the first evening class would only have two students. Because of the deranged behavior of her father, Roger Blount would no longer be studying with his friends.

She didn't have to wait long for Diane to enter the room or for her students to arrive. She'd seen both Clint and Parker from a distance, but seeing them close up almost took her breath away. It was evident, they were still building up their muscles they'd lost when they were on the slave ranch in Mexico. She'd heard how they had been branded, just like Jerilyn's friend, Peter. Assessing them, she noticed they each wore long sleeved shirts, rolled up to their elbows. Were they ashamed of the marks that signified their status as slaves? She hoped that wasn't the case. Everyone had scars even though they weren't all visible.

While she'd been silently thinking about the young men she would be teaching, they took their seats and opened the book from which they'd been studying.

"Good evening," Diane greeted them. "I'm so exciting to introduce Josie Rawlins to you. She's a trained teacher and is going to be taking over the class as soon as she is comfortable with our study plan."

Josie could tell, just by the look in the eyes of these men that they were skeptical of her, because of her father's actions. She decided this was the time to set the record straight about who and what she was.

"That's right, I'm Josie Rawlins. My brother Jake was brought up here. He also lost his life here. What I wouldn't give to have found him alive, but that was not to be. All the years since my brother disappeared my father has fed off the hate, he had for the people who stole him away from us. When we learned Jake died on this ranch at the hands of the Hendersons, he transferred his hate to this ranch, especially after he heard the Hendersons had been found guilty and sent to one of the penal colonies. It was that hatred that caused my brother, Zander, to rustle your cattle and to set fire to one of your barns. It was also that hatred that caused my father to take the life of your friend, Roger, and to wound several others at the same time. I want you to know I am not my father. I do not condone the actions of either him or my older brother. I never knew Jake. I was just a baby when he disappeared. Both my mother and I were preparing to leave my brother and father to start a new life. We were sick of the abuse.

"Now that I've had my say, I've been hired to teach. I'm delighted to think that the two of you will be my first students."

~ * ~

Clint left class with mixed emotions. He wanted to hate Josie because of what her father and brother did to Resurrection Ranch. Because of them, Roger was dead, to say nothing about those who were injured. They'd also lost one of their barns along with twenty-five head of prize cattle. At the same time, he felt an attraction to Josie. Maybe it was because she was the first woman his age to pay any attention to him.

"You look like a lovesick calf," Parker teased. "Are you having fantasies about our new teacher?"

"Don't even go there. We both know who she is. If they hadn't come here, Roger would still be with us."

"She didn't pull the trigger on that laser pistol. It was her father, and if I don't miss my guess, he's mentally unstable. Can't say I condone what he did, but I think I understand it. If I'd found any family, maybe they would have been nuts trying to find out where I was all these years."

"That could be, but you're wrong about me having fantasies about Josie. She's so far above either of us. It's not even funny. She'll never understand what we went through from the time we were brought here until we were rescued."

Clint knew the words he spoke were the truth and yet he prayed the two of them would one day be on the same level.

Together with Parker, he headed toward the dormitory for a good night's sleep. He wondered if his dreams tonight would be the nightmares of the past or pleasant thoughts of what the future could bring.

Chapter Two

Patsy was grateful for the people at Resurrection Ranch who arranged for her to return to Maquoketa to close out their life and prepare to start anew. She knew it would take several days for all of the arrangements to be made. Cassion promised to come for her when she was ready to return to the ranch.

It didn't matter how the trial for her husband, Vern, turned out, she knew she could never return to her life in this town. She was positive the wrongs Vern did on the ranch, including murder, would have reached even to this small town. It wouldn't matter that she had nothing to do with what happened, she would be held responsible and lose any standing she ever had with her friends and even relatives. It was for the best that she sell everything and disappear, just as Jake had over twenty-five years earlier.

"Is that really you, Patsy?" Ellie Blaser called from across the street.

She pasted a smile on her face and waved to Ellie. "Yes, it is. I had to come home to close things out and pack up what belongings we will be needing."

"Close things out?" Ellie questioned, as she crossed the street. "Don't tell me you're leaving again."

"Alright, I won't tell you, but it's for the best. Josie and I need a fresh start. That won't happen here. Everyone must have heard what Vern and Zander did."

Ellie hung her head. "Of course, we have, but we've also heard Vern spewing his hatred ever since Jake disappeared. Everyone in town knew he would explode one day. It's too bad someone had to get killed when it happened. I've known you ever since we started kindergarten together. I can't stand the thought of you leaving here."

Patsy didn't even try to stop the tears that were flowing down her cheeks. "I can't stand the thought of it either. This has been my home all my life, but I can no longer stand to be here. There are too many memories of all the hateful and hurtful things Vern did, not only in this town but also in this house."

"He beat you, didn't he?"

She could only nod her head. "I wanted him to forget all of the hate he was spewing and start living like normal people. He couldn't let it go. He even poisoned Zander's mind with it. Thankfully, the people at Resurrection Ranch forgave my son when he told them where they could find the cattle. In order to make restitution, he agreed to stay on at the ranch and advise them on insurance. They even told him, if he ever wanted to study to do something else, they would make their educational department open to him."

"What about Josie? Why isn't she with you?"

"Even before Vern snapped, she applied to teach at the school on Resurrection Ranch. Once she's trained on their study plan, she will be taking over the classes for the adult students."

Ellie put her arm around Patsy's shoulders and led her across the street to her home. "I can see no reason why you have to stay in the house all by yourself. Mike and I have plenty of room now that we're empty nesters. I can make a fresh pot of coffee. I even made an apple pie this morning. I know how much you love my apple pie."

As Ellie led her across the street, Patsy realized just how exhausted she was from the events of the past several days, coupled with the flight back to Iowa. Since her wrist wasn't completely healed, she dreaded having to prepare her meals on top of everything else that needed to be done. Up until now, Ellie hadn't seen the brace on her wrist. Now she knew she would have to explain her injury to her best friend.

"There's something you need to know," she began.

Ellie waved her hand to indicate she needed Patsy to remain silent. "I saw your brace. Did Vern do this to you?"

"In a way. He was angry that I'd left the apartment and not told him where I was going. He slapped me. When I fell, I braced myself and broke my wrist when I fell. He hit Josie with a clenched fist and broke her jaw. That was just before he lost it completely and shot that young man at the dining hall. It was terrible."

"I'm sure it was, but there's no way anyone would hold you responsible. What are you going to do?"

"I've been offered a position at Resurrection Ranch. I can't believe how understanding and loving those people are. After what Vern did, I was certain they would want all of us arrested and punished for his sins."

"Oh, Patsy, I'm so sorry this is happening to you. Other than giving you a place to stay, what can Mike and I do for you?"

"I-I…" she choked back her sobs. "I was hoping Mike would put the house on the market for me and maybe find a buyer for the business."

"Are you sure this is what you want?"

"Positive. I know what happened to my youngest son. To be truthful, I buried him in my heart long before he died on that ranch. I've met the young men who were his best friends and they are delightful. Knowing what they've been through, it hard to believe they are so well adjusted. I know if it had been me, I'd be mad as a wet hen at everyone and everything."

Ellie led her to the living room and indicated she should sit in the recliner. She didn't think any chair ever felt as good as this one. After she put up her feet, Ellie returned with a cup of steaming coffee and a generous piece of pie.

"Oh dear, if I eat that big a piece of pie, I'll gain a ton of weight."

Ellie laughed at her statement. "Now that's Vern talking. I've heard those words come out of Vern's mouth more than once. Stand up for yourself and eat the pie if that's what you want."

Patsy agreed completely. Those were the words Vern spoke whenever he thought she was eating too much food. He always wanted her to keep the figure she had when they were married two days after she graduated from high school.

~ * ~

Patsy was surprised to see the sun setting in the west when she woke. She had no recollection of falling asleep. The stress of the day must have taken control of her body and mind.

From the kitchen, she could hear Ellie and Mike talking in hushed tones. She knew they were discussing her and the reason she returned to Maquoketa. Although she wasn't comfortable with being the topic of conversation, she put her fears behind her and walked out to the kitchen to join them.

"I thought you were still sleeping," Mike greeted her.

"I was, but if I sleep the day away, I won't sleep tonight. I'm certain Ellie must have told you I want to put the house on the market."

"She did, but are you certain about that? I mean, what if Vern doesn't want everything sold?"

"He has no say in it. If he isn't sent to a mental institution, he'll spend the rest of his life in prison. He killed a man and wounded several others. That's not something that is easily overlooked. If you're not willing to handle the sale, I suppose I can find someone else."

"Nonsense. I just wanted to be sure you knew what you were doing. We can go over there tomorrow and do a walkthrough. With the way the housing market is now, I doubt we'll have much trouble in finding a buyer for it. As for the business, I've been hearing a lot of gossip about what's going to happen to it. I heard from an insurance agency in Des Moines. It seems they want to open a branch office and wondered what was going on with Vern's office. I told them I didn't know but I do have their contact information."

Although Patsy thought she would feel relief at knowing someone had already voiced an interest in the business, it did tug at her heartstrings. The insurance agency had been part of her life ever since she and Vern married almost thirty years ago. The thought of someone else handling Vern's long-time customers and sitting in the office where her husband and son worked for so many years was difficult.

"That all sounds good. I worked with the legal department for the ranch and they got Vern to sign over power of attorney to me. I'm certain he knew there was no way he would ever be able to return here and resume his position in the community. He sealed his fate the moment he packed his laser pistol before we left for Resurrection Ranch. It was bound to happen sooner rather than later. I'm just ashamed to say he took the life of one of Jake's friends in the process."

"What do you want to do with the furnishings in the house?" Ellie asked.

"Most of them will have to be sold. The apartments are completely furnished. There are a few pieces I want to take with me and others I want to put into storage. The people at the ranch assured me they have built some storage buildings, as others have things that they want to put away until the houses can be built. They will arrange for our things to be moved. What I need to do is pack up our clothes and take them with me when I return. Of course, that won't be until the house as well as the business have been sold and the final payments have been signed."

Patsy knew from the look on Ellie's face that her friend disapproved of her plans, but that wouldn't stop her from carrying out her agenda.

~ * ~

As soon as they finished breakfast the next morning, Patsy crossed the street with Ellie and Mike to do a walkthrough of the house she'd called home for so many years. For a moment she stood on the wrap around porch reliving both happy and sad memories before she put the key into the lock.

The front door opened and squeaked, as it always had in the past. It was familiar and yet so different from the modern doors that slid open at a voice command or the touch of your hand on the pad beside the door. Like most of the homes in this town, she knew it was old fashioned. Whoever purchased the house would, more than likely, completely gut the interior and make it into a more modern version of itself. She didn't want to think about what would happen once her name was no longer on the deed.

Inside, everything was just as she'd left it when they went to Nevada. The clocks still registered the right time, all of the furnishings were in their proper place. It saddened her to see the thin layer of dust that covered her tables as well as the mantle.

In her mind's eye, she could see the living room decorated for Christmas. From the mantle there were three stockings hung. Even though Jake hadn't been there for more than twenty years, she still hung his stocking along with those for Zander and Jodie every year.

She turned her gaze to the open staircase leading to the second story and she could see Zander and Jake racing down on Christmas morning to see what Santa left in their stockings as well as under the decorated Christmas tree.

Her mind told her this was all in the past and her future no longer revolved around these few rooms of furniture. They belonged in another lifetime, another era.

Suddenly, it was all too much for her. Before her eyes, the room began to spin, and a warm darkness encompassed her entire being.

The electronic grandfather's clock was chiming eleven when she again opened her eyes. To her surprise, she was lying on the sofa in the living room, with her friends hovering over her.

"You gave us quite a scare," Ellie said. "Mike called the paramedics. They should be here soon."

"Y-you shouldn't have done that," she stammered. "It was just all too overwhelming coming back here. Too many memories."

Sirens sounded from outside the house, cutting off any further conversation. Within moments, the room was filled with medical personnel.

"Just let us check you over, Mrs. Rawlins," a young man in the uniform of a city paramedic said.

She recognized him as Paul Fredrick. Had Jake not been taken from them, she was certain he and Paul would have become fast friends, as they were the same age.

"I'm fine, really I am."

"Mr. Blaser said you passed out. We need to check you over."

Reluctantly, she allowed him to take her blood pressure and other vitals. As he did, he tapped the numbers into his communicator.

"Your blood pressure is too low and your pulse is too fast. The doctor wants us to bring you into the hospital for evaluation."

She knew better than to argue with anyone over the decision. If she did, she knew Ellie and Mike would have insisted on her going to the hospital.

"Don't worry about a thing here, Patsy," Mike said. "I'll take the pictures I need and lock up when I leave. You can decide on the furnishings later."

She nodded and allowed Paul to help her to the gurney to take her out to the air ambulance. It reminded her of when she'd been taken to the hospital on Resurrection Ranch two weeks earlier.

"Have you passed out before this?" Paul answered, once they lifted off for the flight to the hospital.

"I was assaulted by my husband and lost consciousness. That was also when I broke my wrist."

"Do you know the name of the doctor who treated you at Resurrection Ranch?"

"It was Dr. Gratan."

Paul nodded his head as though he recognized the name. She didn't think it was possible, but in this day and age names of prominent physicians could be well known.

Chapter Three

Josie stared at her communicator in disbelief. How could her mother have been hospitalized in Maquoketa? She'd been fine when she left yesterday. How could this have happened?

Rather than communicate with her mother, she messaged Ellie. Just last night her mother told her she was staying with Ellie and Mike. It came as a surprise, considering the house was still completely furnished.

Ellie's face immediately filled the screen of her communicator. "What happened to Mom?" Josie asked as soon as the connection was completed.

"We went over for a walkthrough of the house. I think it was just too much for her. She collapsed and lost consciousness. Mike was concerned and called the paramedics. They insisted she go to the hospital. I could see that she was reluctant, but she didn't argue with them."

"Do I need to get transportation to Iowa to be with her?"

"No, I'm sure they won't keep her long. It was precautionary. Be assured Mike and I will take good care of her."

"Is Mike listing the house for Mom?"

"Yes, and he thinks he has a buyer for the business. He was approached by an agency out of Des Moines when they heard about what happened with your dad and Zander in Nevada. They wanted to open a branch and take over your dad's clients. We told your mother about it. Once she's out of the hospital they will come here to meet with her and negotiate a proper price."

Although Josie knew selling the house as well as the business was the reason her mother returned to Iowa, the thought of it actually happening hit her hard. She knew she would have to advise Zander of what was going on, but for now she had to come to grips with it herself.

After the connection was broken, she went to find Zander. He needed to know what was going on back home.

She found Zander working in Mark's office, organizing the files that had been left by the Hendersons.

"I didn't expect to see you here, Sis. Don't you have a class to prepare for?"

"For now, the prep is being done for me. I'm just monitoring until Diane feels I'm ready to take over. That will probably be the first of next week. I just had a message from Ellie Blaser. Mom is in the hospital."

"Hospital? What happened?"

"She was talking to Mike about listing our house and they were doing a walkthrough when Mom collapsed. Ellie thinks it was all too much for her. She's still recovering from what happened with Dad. Ellie also said that Mike has had an offer from an agency in Des Moines to buy the business from her. Since she has power of attorney…" Josie stopped midsentence when she saw the look on her brother's face. "Are you okay with it?"

Zander nodded. "I just didn't think things would happen so quickly. Of course, I understand that our clients need someone to take care of them. I was a fool to listen to Dad and take part in his plan to get revenge for something that happened so many years ago."

"Don't beat yourself up too badly about it. We both grew up listening to Dad spew his hateful words. I wasn't as affected as you were, mainly because I was younger and didn't remember Jake. With you it was different. You were old enough to remember him. It's no wonder you fed into everything Dad told you."

"You're right of course. I do remember Jake. I don't know if it's because I actually remember him or that Dad insisted, I remember him. If it wasn't for the pictures on the wall of the family room, I doubt I could even tell you what he looked like."

"Are you going to be alright?"

"I will be as soon as I know that Mom has been released from the hospital. I'm worried about her ability to handle the sale of the house and the business. She's been through a lot in the past couple of months."

Josie agreed with her brother. They had all been through a rough time. She was relieved to have been accepted by the people at the ranch. She wouldn't have faulted any of them if they'd pressed charges against

Zander. They could have also forced her and her mother to leave immediately. It was evident everyone here was engaged in bringing about the resurrection of not only the ranch but all of the people who lived and worked here.

~ * ~

After Josie left to go back to the educational facility, Zander took a few moments to digest what she'd just told him. He wished he could be with his mom while she dealt with things at home. When she told him what she was planning to do, he worried about her returning to Iowa, but as part of his deal to avoid prosecution for the theft of the cattle as well as the arson to the barn he promised not to leave the ranch for at least a year.

Although he wasn't a prisoner, he knew better than to go back on his word. There was enough acreage for him to explore so that he didn't feel confined. He did enjoy riding the horses and was looking forward to participating in the architectural training Mark's Uncle David was starting as soon as the classes could be scheduled.

He thought about how he felt knowing the business would soon be sold. It would no longer be known as Rawlins and Son Insurance. He couldn't put voice to his feelings. The agency was supposed to be his future and yet now, he knew it wasn't exactly what he wanted to do with his life. So much had changed in the past few months, he was completely reevaluating his life path for the future.

"Is something wrong?"

Zander looked up to see Mark enter the office. "I'm not sure. You know Mom went back to Iowa to put the house on the market. I'm afraid it was too much for her. She collapsed and was taken to the hospital. Thank goodness her best friend and her husband are there to help her."

"I think it might be best if we talk to Cassion and Dr. Gratan about this. It's possible Cassion can get away to go up there and help her out. I know he was talking about going back there to see if he can locate either Foster Warren or Noah Hammer. They were former residents of Henderson Ranch who were kidnapping kids and selling them to

Henderson. They were working for Henderson, just like Delos Reynolds was. We knew that Delos didn't sell any kids after he brought Peter here, because Peter's dad killed him. We also learned that the other two were instrumental in bringing the three younger boys here. They were foster children and their parents couldn't be found."

Zander felt his stomach drop. He'd heard the name of Delos Reynolds in conjunction with the kidnapping of his brother. Knowing there were others doing the same thing as recently as when the three younger boys were brought here, made him think he was going to be sick. If the two men Mark mentioned were still stealing children, how much deeper would the investigation of the running of Henderson Ranch go?

He remembered the files he'd been working on when Josie came to see him. On the top of the pile were the files for Jake, Roger, Clint and Parker. He'd read Jake's file over and over again trying to understand why his brother had been taken from his family. Since being here, he'd been told many of the boys whose families hadn't been found, were either orphans or were in foster care. Had Jake been taken for an entirely different reason? Was it possible because his brother was vulnerable or maybe Delos Reynolds was nothing more than an opportunist, taking a child who seemed to be alone, without researching the family any further?

He sat aside his brother's file and picked up the one for Roger. It didn't make any difference who took him, or why, considering he was already dead. He'd skimmed through it enough to realize Roger hadn't been kidnapped, but had been turned over to the state of Nevada because they thought sending him to Henderson Ranch was the best decision. At the time they had no idea of what was going on under their noses. They were also paying Henderson to carry out his abuse and forced labor of those unfortunate enough to be placed in his care.

Setting aside the first two files, he picked up the one marked Clint Anders. Opening it up, he turned to the last pages. The picture of Clint at the age of three, reminded him of Jake, before he disappeared.

Rather than continue to dwell on the picture, he read about how he came to be one of Henderson's slave laborers.

Clint Anders arrived at the ranch this morning accompanied by Noah Hammer. Hammer told me that the boy was in an abusive situation living with his dirty whore mother, in Des Moines, Iowa. Noah was offered ten thousand dollars for the boy. He insisted on getting fifteen thousand dollars because he was the one taking the risks of procuring the boys for me. We finally agreed on twelve thousand five hundred dollars. I certainly hope he is worth the money I had to pay to get him. In the future I will have to be careful to see that Foster and Delos don't get wind of what I paid Noah. I don't need to have them asking for more money.

From what Zander heard Delos brought Peter to Henderson and received over twice the amount of money paid for Clint. He wondered how that could have been. In this day and age of everything being computerized, how could the state not have known about the inhuman treatment received by the children entrusted to the care of the Hendersons. Especially, when the state was paying them for training them to become little more than slave labor.

Curiosity got the better of him and he opened the file for Peter. He immediately turned to the last pages that detailed his arrival at the ranch.

Delos drives a hard bargain. He wants thirty thousand for this kid, Peter. I decided it's probably worth it, because he's relatively healthy and the birth father signed away his parental rights because he can't care for the kid and the mother is a dirty whore. I hope he's worth the price. Hopefully, he'll be a good ranch hand and I'll be able to get top dollar for him in Mexico after he turns eighteen. When I questioned Delos about the price he wanted, he said the father wanted to get twenty thousand dollars, considering he was signing away his parental rights. That's a lot better than some of those kids from foster care. Thank goodness Delos isn't asking for more money like Noah and Foster.

Zander thought he was going to be physically sick. The very thought of what Jake suffered at the hands of kidnappers before he ended up under Henderson's control made him want to vomit. His father was right about the inhumanity of this place, but that was behind everyone who returned to Resurrection Ranch. From now on he decided he would work with everyone here to make amends for the evil associated with Mr. and Mrs. Henderson.

~ * ~

"Do you think you should go to Iowa?" Hodia asked, once she and Cassion were alone in their apartment.

"From what I heard from Josie and Zander; I think it's the right thing to do. It's not just for Patsy Rawlins, but I've had a lead on Foster Warren. The Chicago Complex says they have heard about someone by the name of Fredrick Warren living in Keokuk, Iowa. He's the right age and description from the last pictures we have of him in Hendersons' files. I have to make certain this is our man. If I can be of help to Patsy, so much the better."

"That's what I was hoping you'd say. I know it will put Josie's mind at ease. She's ready to start taking over the early morning and late afternoon classes. Added to that she's just not strong enough to make the trip. I have your bag packed, so you can leave first thing tomorrow morning."

Cassion hugged her tightly. As much as she wanted Cassion to stay here with her, she knew he needed to be with Patsy and to find out if the man by the name of Fredrick Warren was the same man who kidnapped so many children and brought them to Henderson Ranch. If he was that man, she knew Cassion would see to his arrest. It was definitely the right thing to do. Noah and Foster were the last two links to the horrific past that was Henderson Ranch.

Chapter Four

Cassion's flight from Nevada to Iowa was uneventful. As much as he wanted to find if Frederick Warren and Foster Warren were one in the same, he knew he had to see Patsy Rawlins first. He'd promised Zander and Josie he would make certain everything was okay before continuing on to do the duty he'd been assigned.

He wondered how he'd become involved in this mess. As a lawyer, he was more comfortable in the courtroom. His job was to prosecute law breakers not track them down. He decided it would be best to involve the local police force before he confronted Warren, since he had no idea how the man would react to having his DNA chip read and his finger prints taken.

The hover craft pilot announced they were ready to dock and Cassion steeled himself for the inevitable meeting with Patsy. In his heart he knew he should have never left her here alone days earlier. She was too fragile from the attack she'd suffered at the hands of her husband. Returning to the home she shared with him for so many years could have triggered bad memories. It was entirely possible she'd been abused by him throughout their marriage.

As soon as the docking procedures were finished, Cassion picked up his carry-on bag and prepared to meet with Patsy Rawlins and her friends.

To his surprise, he was met by a man who appeared to be close to Patsy's age. He was dressed casually, not at all what he expected to see, since from what he'd heard Mike Blaser was a real estate agent. Considering this was midday on a work day, he'd expected to see the man wearing a business suit. Of course, he was used to life in the larger cities. Maquoketa was in a rural area. It was entirely possible the people here were more casual.

"You must be Cassion," the man said, extending his hand. "I'm

Mike Blaser. My wife told me you would be arriving and asked me to meet you. She's over at the hospital with Patsy."

Cassion was shocked to hear that Patsy was still hospitalized. "Is something seriously wrong with her?"

Mike shook his head. "She's being treated by their family doctor. He's a bit old school and likes to err on the side of caution. He's treated just about everyone in this town from cradle to grave. In other words, he has prescribed rest and she's getting plenty of it in the hospital. If you ask me, Vern has been abusing her for years and she's been running on tension for a long time. He's been nothing but a pain in the ass ever since Jake went missing. I tolerated him, because Patsy and my wife Ellie have been lifelong friends. He's also the only insurance agent in town. If it had been up to me, I would have cut ties with him years ago."

"I wondered about the abuse. Although Patsy said it was the first time, I wasn't so sure about that. From what I've ascertained, Vern Rawlins is an angry and violent man. That said, do you think I'll be able to see Patsy?"

"She's looking forward to seeing you as well. It will do her a world of good to hear how her kids are doing. I know you didn't come all the way here just to check on Patsy. Do you have a lead on the people who have been kidnapping boys like Jake?"

"From what we've learned there were three former residents of Henderson Ranch who were supplying boys. The one who kidnapped Jake was murdered well over twenty years ago. I have a lead on someone in this area who might be one of the others who were supplying Henderson. Once I'm certain Patsy is going to be okay, I'll be heading out to a little town called Keokuk. Have you heard of it?"

Mike nodded. "It's about a hundred and sixty miles from here. I'd be happy to take you."

Cassion appreciated the offer. In a town as small as this one, he doubted if he would be able to rent a hover craft for the flight to Keokuk. Even with his status, he couldn't make something like that appear out of nowhere.

~ * ~

Patsy wanted nothing more than to get out of this hospital bed and finishing closing up her life in Maquoketa, so she could return to Nevada and see how her children were doing. Ellie promised to be here when the doctor made his rounds so, she could take her back to the house.

"I'm sorry I didn't get here earlier, but Mike got a call from Zander this morning asking him to go out to the hover port and meet Cassion's flight. Isn't he the alien lawyer from Resurrection Ranch?"

"He is. I hope there's nothing wrong with Zander and Josie."

"I don't think so. It's possible he's here to see how you are doing."

Patsy breathed a sigh of relief. She didn't think she was important enough to take Cassion away from his duties at the ranch, but she was honored to have him visit her none the same.

Within a matter of minutes, Cassion and Mike entered her room.

"It's good to see you, Patsy," Cassion greeted her. "Zander and Josie send their love."

"I can't believe you came all this way just to tell me that, although I do appreciate your visit."

"You're right, I do have another reason for coming to Iowa. You're aware that the man who kidnapped your son was murdered over twenty years ago. We have a lead on another one of the men who were taking children to work on Henderson Ranch. He's in this area and your friend, Mike, has agreed to take me there."

She nodded, more grateful for Mike and Ellie than ever. "I hope this doesn't turn out to be a wild goose chase."

It took a moment for her words to register with Cassion. When they did, he smiled. "We're dedicated to checking out any lead we get about the monsters who kidnapped those children. We know that as of five years ago they were perpetuating these crimes and they need to be punished. Even if the lead turns out to be false, my being here is also to put Zander and Josie's minds at ease."

"I do thank you for everything you've done for my family. With everything Zander and Vern did to your people, you have been more than generous."

Before they could continue their conversation, the doctor came into the room. "I hope I'm not interrupting anything, but I've checked out all of the tests that you've had, Patsy, and I agree with you. Rest is what you need, but not here. Ellie and Mike will make certain you get the rest you need, until your business here is finished. At that time, you'll be free to return to Nevada. I have to say you will be missed here in Maquoketa. I've known you since you were a child. I do agree with you that this is what's best for you and the kids. Just make certain you stay in touch. I don't want to lose a good friend."

"Thank you. I do need to get away from here, not because of my friends, but because of the memories of everything that has happened since Jake disappeared. Even though he lived for twelve years after he was taken, I knew he was dead two weeks after we lost him. Unlike Vern, I tried to go on and give our children a good life. He wanted to raise them with the hatred he held in his heart. It's over now and it's time for Zander, Josie and me to start new lives."

~ * ~

After leaving the hospital, Cassion was anxious to go to Keokuk and meet with the man he thought was Foster Warren. He prayed to the One God that the lead he'd been given was the right one.

The trip to Keokuk was an interesting one. Having the time to talk to Mike was enlightening. It was good to see Patsy and her children through the eyes of one of her good friends. He thought he knew the entire story, but what he learned from Mike was a completely different story.

While Zander was his first born, he was not the favored son. From the moment Jake entered the world, Vern doted on his younger son. It was as though Zander had, somehow, disappointed his father. Mike thought it was because Zander was more interested in sports than in the education Vern desired, he pursue. Once Jake went missing, Vern did nothing but spout hatred. When Zander got a chance to play football at a local college, Vern insisted the boy study to get his insurance license and join him in the family business. Even though Zander was one of the top agents in the state, Mike knew his heart wasn't in it. He was doing it only to please the father who had always loved his younger brother more than him.

"What about Josie? She went to college."

"It certainly wasn't what Vern wanted. Patsy went to work at the diner to pay for Josie's education. Vern said the only one of his children who deserved to go to college was Jake. He certainly didn't want Patsy to go to work. They had some real knock down drag 'em out fights about it. I should know since we live across the street from them. After those fights, Patsy would wear a lot of heavy makeup. It was evident he was beating on her, but up until now, she never admitted to it. They had good social standing and I'm certain he wanted to perpetuate that image, even if it wasn't true."

Cassion was pleased to know more of the story behind the newest residents of Resurrection Ranch. They were survivors, only in a different way, from the other young men and children who decided to make the ranch part of their future.

The city limits of Keokuk loomed on the horizon. In no time at all, Mike landed his craft at a well-maintained house on a quiet street. "This is where the information you gave me says that Warren lives."

Cassion was conflicted about this meeting. He wasn't certain if this was the man he was looking for, and if it was, he would have to involve the local law enforcement agency to make the actual arrest. His legal expertise was in the courtroom.

At the front door of the house, Mike announced who they were and why they were there. The woman who answered the door identified herself as Lynette Warren.

"We're looking for Foster Warren," Cassion said, once they were invited into the house.

"You should talk to my husband. Foster is his brother. Can I get you a cup of coffee and some freshly made pecan pie?"

Mike accepted her offer. While Cassion had no idea what pecan pie was, he was certainly willing to try it. He'd left the ranch right after breakfast and eaten only a light lunch before leaving to make the trip from Maquoketa to Keokuk. His stomach was ready to growl in anticipation of having something to put into it.

Before she could return with the pie and coffee, an older man in a wheelchair entered the room. "I'm Fredrick Warren," he said.

"We're looking for Foster Warren."

Fredrick had a pained expression on his face. "What has my twin brother done now?"

"Twin?" Cassion questioned.

"We're not identical twins, by any stretch of the imagination. I call him my evil twin. He's been in more trouble than I could ever imagine doing."

"I'm here from Resurrection Ranch," Cassion began. "In going over the records from Henderson Ranch, we've learned that your brother has been kidnapping children and selling them to Henderson for slave labor."

Frederick wheeled himself across the room to sit facing them, while Cassion and Mike occupied the couch. "It's a long story. Let's wait until Lynette brings in the pie and coffee."

As though on cue, Lynette entered the room with a tray containing four plates of pie as well as four cups of steaming coffee.

As much as Cassion wanted to learn the truth, he politely tried a taste of the pie and deemed it to be absolutely delicious. He would have to remember to ask Connor and Julie if they could add it to the menu in the future.

"Everything started when Foster and I were four years old. Our mother died in childbirth and our father was so devastated he committed suicide. At the time we were living in Nevada. The child protective services placed us on Henderson Ranch. At that time, it was run by Theo's father and mother. They were wonderful people. We were brought up with their son, Theo, as well as Delos Reynolds and Noah Hammer. There were other kids there, but the four of us were the same age. Unlike what Henderson Ranch became when Theo inherited it, the food, as well as the education was first rate. I swear Mr. and Mrs. Henderson were angels sent by the One God.

"When we aged out of the program, we were all offered scholarships to go to the University of Nevada, by the state. I wanted the education, but Theo said he wanted to run the ranch. As for Noah, Delos and Foster, they wanted no part of higher education. I should tell you the education would have been wasted on Delos. He wasn't the brightest bulb in the pack, if you get my meaning. Noah and Foster weren't far behind him.

"For several years, I lost track of all of them, including my brother. When the news about the raid on Henderson Ranch and the trial for Theo and his wife came to light, Foster contacted me. He said he knew that Delos was dead and he would be too, if anyone knew where he was and what he'd done. I told him I didn't want to know what was going on and suggested he lose my information. After that I didn't hear anything more from him, although my communicator tracked the information of where he was calling from to Indianapolis, Indiana."

Although Frederic's story was believable, Cassion wanted proof of what the man told him. "Do you have proof about your being a twin?"

"I do. Honey, would you bring in the file with our important papers?"

Lynette left the room and Frederick returned his attention to Mike and Cassion. "Lynette has become my legs since I was in the accident. It happened at work several years ago. I was a researcher at a chemical plant in St. Louis, Missouri. There was an explosion and I lost the use of my legs. The company fast tracked my disability claim and gave me a generous pension. It was enough to buy this house and move here. This is where my wife grew up and it was the perfect place for us to relocate. I still do side work for them via my communicator, but I can no longer do what I was trained to do."

Lynette returned to the room with a folder marked, Fredrick's documents. Cassion looked over the first document that listed Frederick and Foster as fraternal twins. The next ones were the death certificates for both of their parents, along with the papers sending them to Henderson Ranch.

"I watched Theo's trial and couldn't believe what he'd turned the ranch into. It made me sick to my stomach, I didn't want to even admit I knew him as a kid."

"What about Paul Grainger?" Cassion inquired.

"Paul lived with his father on the ranch. Art Granger was the foreman, but Paul didn't want anything to do with ranching. He aged out before we did and moved into town. They were opening a new hover craft factory there and he got a job right away. I watched his trial too, but to be truthful, I wouldn't have recognized him, if I met him on the street. As I recall, he was a real piece of work. He could be your best friend to your face and stab you in the back if you weren't watching his every step."

"Did you know his wife, Doreen?"

"She was one of the girls from town. As I recall, she was one of the most popular girls in town. The Henderson's sent us there for high school. She was a senior when we were freshmen. You know the kind, prom queen, head cheerleader. I could hardly believe she married Paul, but there she was at the trial, just as guilty as he was. She could have had the world on a silver platter, but she settled for a line worker at the hover craft factory. Guess brains and beauty don't always come in the same package.

"Can you tell me what my brother has done that brings someone like you out to Iowa?"

"According to the records at Resurrection Ranch, Delos Reynolds, Noah Hammer and your brother were actively kidnapping children and selling them to Henderson. They were getting ten to fifteen thousand dollars for every boy they brought there. You wouldn't have a recent photo of your brother, would you?"

"I'd like to say no, but I do have his image saved on my communicator from when he contacted me. I actually printed it off and framed it. You know, a remembrance of my twin."

Without being told, Lynette left the room. From somewhere in the house, Cassion could hear a printer. She was probably making a copy of the picture.

When she returned to the room, she handed the copy of the picture to Cassion. It was amazing and yet not unexpected to see the resemblance between Frederick and his brother, Foster.

"Thank you. I don't like putting you in the position of providing information about your brother. It can't be easy. I know I wouldn't want to have to turn in my brother for something he did. Luckily, he has a very important position on the dark side of the moon. We don't see each other often, but we are in constant contact on a monthly basis. You have lost far too much in this life. I pray once this is finally over, you and your wife will live the quiet life you deserve."

Cassion left the Warren home with mixed emotions. How could two brothers be so entirely different from one another? Looking at the picture there was definitely a close resemblance, but that was where it stopped. While Frederick was a mild-mannered scientist, Foster looked as though life had hardened him and perhaps warped his perception of right and wrong.

Chapter Five

Patsy was relieved to be able to leave the hospital. She knew better than go back to the home that she once shared with Vern and their children. There were too many memories there, both good and bad. Luckily, Mike had a buyer for the house as well as the business. He even suggested an auction house where she could dispose of the furniture, she wasn't taking to Nevada with her.

The offer for the agency had been more than generous. It helped that she knew the man who made the offer and was positive he would look out for the best interests of the clients her husband and son serviced for so many years.

As for the house, it had been a young couple with small children who fell in love with it the first time they toured it. She knew they would be happy there. The memories of Jake and the years after his disappearance wouldn't haunt them the way they did her.

"I can't believe you're planning to leave tomorrow," Ellie lamented.

"I've done what I came to do. I can't thank Mike enough for finalizing everything for me so quickly. I need to get back to the kids and start my new life. I'm excited about training with Connor and Julie to become one of the chefs at the ranch. It will be so much more rewarding than waiting tables at the diner. Besides, I'll have enough money from the sale of the house, furnishings and the business to live comfortably. Even if I didn't have a job to return to, I could live comfortably."

"What about the money for Vern's defense?"

"There is no defense. A room full of people saw him snap and kill that young man as well as wound several others. Cassion thinks he will probably be sent to a mental institution for the rest of his life. I'm not so much of a hypocrite as to grieve for his loss. Even before all of this happened, I'd decided to divorce him. I could no longer take the abuse.

The only thing I regret is that I will no longer be living across the street from my best friend."

Ellie dabbed at her eye with a tissue. "It doesn't matter where we live. Nothing will ever break our friendship. I intend to blow up your communicator every day so we can stay in touch. No matter what, you are my best friend and I refuse to lose contact with you. Don't forget that Josie is my Goddaughter. I won't abandon her either."

"I know. Nothing will ever separate us for one another. For now, let's go out and do some major shopping. I shipped the kids' stuff to them, but I think I deserve a new wardrobe to start my new life. I need to get rid of all the things that remind me of Vern and the life we lived here."

~ * ~

Josie was surprised when the box containing her belongings, was delivered to the apartment she shared with her mother. She'd wondered what would happen to the things she'd left behind in Iowa. At the time they came to Nevada, she didn't know they would never return to Iowa. With everything that happened, she knew she couldn't face her family and friends again.

Rather than open the box, she left the apartment and went out for a walk. Being Saturday, she didn't have to think about school. To be truthful, she wanted to be alone more than anything else.

"You look like you're deep in thought," Clint said from behind her.

She turned abruptly and almost ran into him. Having him in such close proximity of her came as a surprise. "I-I thought I was alone."

"I didn't mean to startle you," Clint said.

"I-I wasn't startled. I was just thinking about my future."

"That's a coincidence. I was thinking about mine too. It's my day off and I was trying to get the courage to ask you to take a walk with me. I thought maybe we could talk Connor or Julie into packing a picnic lunch for us. I'd like to show you the ranch."

"I don't know how to ride horses," Josie replied, regaining her composure.

"That's too bad. I do know there's an old-fashioned surrey in one of the barns. It's a perfect way to go on a picnic. That way the only one who gets tired out walking is the horse."

She could feel a blush coloring her cheeks. "That sounds delightful."

It also sounds romantic, her inner voice cautioned.

Shut up, she silently admonished.

At home she'd only been allowed to date boys who met with her father's approval. In other words, the sons of the elite members of Maquoketa society. Most of them were the jerky jocks she didn't have time for in high school. They'd been so enamored with their accomplishments in baseball, football, basketball or tennis, she had absolutely nothing in common with them.

Clint was an entirely different person. She'd observed him in class and his intelligence amazed her. For someone who had been denied a formal education, his ability to learn was extraordinary.

Just the thought of spending the day alone with him made her mind race and her entire body tingle.

"I'll go over to the kitchen to see if we can get a picnic basket. Can I pick you up at your apartment in about an hour?"

"I think that would be acceptable. I don't know what to wear for a surrey ride and a picnic."

Clint smiled at her statement. "I like the jeans and top you're wearing now. There's no need to change a thing."

She watched as he walked toward the dining hall. If she didn't know better, she'd think she'd fallen into one of the romance novels she'd studied in contemporary English class in college. Romantic things like this had never happened to her before.

Across the dooryard, she saw Zander coming in her direction. "I saw you talking to Clint," he said when he reached her side. "Is something...?"

"It's none of your business, big brother. Even so, we are going to take a surrey ride to see the ranch and have a picnic."

"Well, it's about time. I know you dated some real losers in the past..."

"Only because they were guys Dad wanted me to date," she interrupted. "Clint is a nice young man and someone I wouldn't mind getting to know. Now, if you'll excuse me, I need to freshen up for my date."

Behind her she could hear Zander chuckling. She knew he was looking out for her best interests, but she was a grown woman and didn't need him to either approve or disapprove of the people in her life.

~ * ~

Clint had been dreaming about Josie for the past few days. He could hardly believe he'd had the good luck to run into her and ask her to go on a picnic with him. Ever since he saw the surrey in one of the outbuildings, he'd been fantasizing about taking Josie out in it. Never in his wildest dreams had he thought she would agree to go out with him.

After a stop at the dining hall to ask about getting a picnic basket, he went out to the corral to choose a horse that would be the perfect one to pull the surrey to the outreaches of the ranch. It was a pasture where the setting was the most beautiful one on the entire acreage.

With the horse hitched to the surrey, he made his way back to the dining hall to pick up the picnic lunch.

"I take it this is for a special lady," Connor said, with a knowing wink.

"You might say that. I asked Miss Josie to go out with me for a tour of the ranch as well as a picnic lunch. I know she's much better than I am, but hopefully, she'll be interested in getting to know me better."

"I wish you luck. I remember feeling the same way about Julie when we first met. She was the most beautiful girl I ever saw. Even though I was already a chef and she was a culinary student, I knew I wanted her in my life. I knew my sister didn't approve of me marrying someone so much younger than me. Her parents thought I was only after her family's money, but that didn't matter. I knew she was the woman I wanted to be with no matter what the repercussions were. It's worked well for us. I hope it does for you too."

Clint didn't agree completely with Connor. Josie was the woman of his dreams, but he didn't fool himself about what the future could hold for either of them. She was her own woman and he had no idea what he wanted to do with the rest of his life.

~ * ~

Josie took one last look in the mirror. She decided to change into a nicer pair of jeans as well as a more flattering top. Even in late September, the Nevada sun could be brutal. Lastly, she chose a sun hat that she'd brought with her from Iowa. With her fair skin, she didn't want the sun to burn her.

As she checked out her outfit, she could hear her father admonish her for not wearing a dress when going out with a young man. Of course, he wouldn't have approved of the young man who was taking her on a tour of the ranch, as well as a picnic. His approval no longer mattered to her. Ever since seeing Clint in class, she found he dominated her dreams both at night and during her waking hours.

After her early morning classes, she was always pleased to see him in either the dining hall or riding out with the other men to work the ranch. She soon learned that he didn't always eat the noon meal in the dining hall, but was glad to see him in class and at the evening meal.

She wished she could talk to her mother about her feelings, but since she wouldn't be leaving for Nevada until tomorrow, that talk would have to wait.

After checking her communicator, she saw it was time to go down to meet Clint. As soon as she saw him, it was evident, he'd changed his clothes. He looked so handsome in the jeans that hugged his hips and the western shirt showed off his sculptured chest and covered the brand she knew he carried on his left upper arm.

"I was able to get a picnic lunch for us," he said, as he helped her get into the surrey. "I hope you enjoy riding in a horse drawn surrey."

"It will be a new experience for me. There aren't many horses back home. I feel like I fell into a historical romance novel."

He looked at her skeptically, as though he had no idea about what she was referencing. She wasn't surprised. With his limited educational background, he was most certainly more concerned with learning about reading, writing and mathematics than works of literature.

"I don't want to come off as ignorant, but what's a historical romance novel?"

She smiled. "It's the kind of book I read in my literature class in college. It will be a while before we're ready to introduce such books into our classes. I'm told that they were read mostly by women and were stories of boy meets girl. Mushy stuff."

"I wouldn't know about that. The way we grew up was being told that all women were dirty whores. I've learned to see things differently since I was rescued. According to my teachers at the Mexico City Complex, women are to be cherished. It's hard to change my thinking, but I'm working on it."

This was the first she'd heard about the teachings of hatred perpetuated on the ranch by the Hendersons. It reminded her of the hatred her father spewed all throughout her life.

"I can understand. All my life I've watched my father's hatred for whoever it was who took my brother, fester. When we learned that Jake lost his life here, he transferred his hatred to this ranch. I didn't agree, but I fed off what he was saying. In my heart I hated this place as much as he did. Now that I've seen all the good that's being done here, I think it's one of the most beautiful places on earth."

"What was it like having parents and an education?"

Clint's question came as a surprise. "I don't know how to answer that. My mother and I were close, but my father only wanted Jake to come home. He tolerated Zander because my brother learned to hate in the same way as my father. As for me, I wasn't the son he lost and I was only a girl. If it had been up to him, I would have never gotten a college education. He didn't believe in women going to college. Mom went to work at the local diner to pay for my education. Even with living at home and the scholarships I received, there were expenses that weren't covered. I'll always be grateful to her for giving me the chance to get an education."

"I'll never be as educated as you are," Clint lamented.

"Don't be so certain about that. I've been monitoring your classes and have just started teaching. You have so much potential, I'm in awe of what you've accomplished in such a short time. By next year at this time, you'll be ready for secondary school classes. I know it seems like things are moving slowly now, but believe me, you are progressing by leaps and bounds."

As though Clint was digesting everything, she just told him, they fell silent for a few minutes. She took the time to revel in the view. From her geography classes, she assumed Nevada was mainly a desert. Instead, she was in awe of the lush grassland and wild flowers that dominated the area.

"I thought this was a desert," she finally said, breaking the silence.

"When we were in Mexico City, contemplating returning to this ranch, one of our teachers told us how the aliens who came here transformed many of the desert areas into lush grasslands. I never questioned it when I was growing up. I just always thought this was one of the prettiest places on the entire ranch. It was in this pasture where your brother went off to find the lost steer. Even though I knew it cost him his life, I always liked coming here. I guess it made me feel closer to him."

In her mind's eye, she could see what Clint was describing. Even though she never knew her brother, she applauded him for going out to find a lost steer. How anyone could have deemed the action punishable was beyond her comprehension.

At last Clint stopped the surrey by a grove of trees. Not far away a small stream of water formed what could be described as a creek.

She watched as he laid out a blanket on the grass and unloaded the contents of the picnic basket. The spread of food contained fried chicken, potato salad, deviled eggs and a bottle of wine. For dessert was a package containing two of the richest brownies she'd ever seen.

They ate in silence, enjoying the delicious food as well as the view.

"I don't want the day to end, but it's getting late," Clint said. "We should get back before they send out a search party for us."

"Are you sure we have to go back. This has been one of the most delightful and relaxing days I can ever remember having."

"We do, if we don't want to miss the evening meal. Besides, the mentors are pretty strict about curfews. The little kids have to be in by nine on the weekends and eight on school nights. With as early as the days start on the ranch, I like to be in bed by nine, ten at the latest. Being able to sleep in a comfortable bed and look forward to a good meal the next morning is very important to me."

She completely understood. As a kid, her father insisted on early bedtimes. The only exception had been when she went to her senior prom. Even then he'd been sitting up waiting for her to return home when her date dropped her off at two in the morning.

Reluctantly, she helped him pack up the leftovers and fold the blanket. She prayed this wouldn't be the last time the two of them were able to be alone together.

~ * ~

The stares from everyone in the dining hall were not missed by Clint. He knew once he returned to the dormitory, he would have to endure the teasing of his friends, but he didn't mind. Being with Josie for the past few hours was worth it.

Her advanced education didn't seem to matter when they were together. She wasn't his teacher, just a desirable woman who seemed interested in everything he told her about ranching. She even asked him if he would teach her how to ride a horse. In his wildest dreams he never thought he would be able to teach her anything. He certainly didn't consider riding a horse anything that needed to be taught. He'd been riding horses for as long as he could remember.

Even though they selected a secluded table, Cassion sought them out and asked if he could join them.

"I'm sorry to barge in on the two of you like this, but may I join you?" Cassion asked.

"Of course," Josie replied.

Clint knew he wouldn't have been as eager with the answer. Of course, he knew Cassion returned from Iowa last week and would have news about Josie's mother.

"As you know, I went to Iowa last week. I had a line on the man who kidnapped Parker."

The mention of the man who changed his friend's life forever when he was little more than a toddler, piqued his attention. "You know who he is?"

"We found his name in the file about Parker. His name is Foster Warren. I found a man, in Keokuk, Iowa, by the name of Frederick Warren. I was certain he was Foster using an assumed name. It turned out the man was Foster's twin brother and they had both been raised by Theodore Henderson's father. At that time this was a reputable boys ranch. They were raised with the Mr. Henderson you knew, Noah Hammer and Delos Reynolds."

"Does Parker know about this?" Clint asked.

"I met with him this afternoon and he wanted me to tell you about what I found as well."

Cassion paused and Clint studied the expression on Josie's face.

"The monster who took my brother was raised on this ranch? Didn't he know what a hell hole he was taking Jake to?"

"When the original kids were here, things were much different, or at least that's what Frederick told me. He also said they were given a good education and allowed to attend high school in town. When they all turned eighteen, they were offered scholarships to the University of Nevada. Frederick was the only one who took them up on the offer.

"That said, he was able to give me an idea of where to look for his brother. I contacted our operatives in Indiana and they have a lead on where Foster is living. I have to leave tomorrow morning to check it out. Do the two of you think you can go to Las Vegas and meet Patsy's flight? I checked, and you do have your pilot's license, Josie. I wouldn't ask, but I don't want Foster to get wind of our plans and disappear again."

"I can understand Josie going, but why do you want me to go with her?" Clint inquired.

"Even though it's not a long trip, I don't want her going alone. There will also be luggage to load and I thought the two of you might enjoy having some together before it's time for classes to start again on Monday."

"What about church?" Josie asked.

"That won't be a problem. Her flight isn't due in until three tomorrow afternoon. With church in the morning, you'll be able to leave right after the noon meal and still be there on time."

For the first time in his life, Clint wanted to jump for joy, but he didn't act on his impulse. Any fears he harbored about not being able to be alone with Josie in the future dissolved. Tomorrow would be another day when she wouldn't be his teacher, but a woman who held his interest.

~ * ~

After Clint left Josie at the apartment Complex, she stood outside watching him cross the short distance to the dormitory. It had been a delightful day and the thought of the two of them flying to Las Vegas tomorrow to pick up her mother excited her so much, she didn't know if she'd be able to sleep tonight.

To her surprise, she was joined by Caroline Phillips. Days earlier, she'd told her mother how much she wanted to meet the woman considered a national treasure because of her personal knowledge of history.

"Josie," Caroline said. "Can we talk for a few minutes?"

In her wildest dreams, she never expected Caroline to seek her out. "Of course, we can."

"I saw you with Clint and I wanted to give you a bit of motherly advice. I know your mother is in Iowa and I thought maybe you'd want someone older to talk to."

"I was thinking the same thing earlier in the day. I've never been on a date because someone wanted to be with me."

"I don't understand. You're a beautiful woman. Surely, you've been on dates before."

"I wanted to go away to school, but my father insisted I could get the same education at the local college and continue to live at home. As for dates, they were always ones that were set up by my dad. He wanted me to date and possibly marry the sons of his influential friends. They were all jerky jocks who couldn't talk about anything but their achievements on the sporting fields. I wanted more."

"Did you find it with Clint?"

"Surprisingly, I did. I was afraid my educational background would be a stumbling block between the two of us, but we found so many things to talk about."

"I thought as much when I saw the two of you together at the evening meal. It was the same when I first met Aaron. Even though I'd been in suspended animation for a hundred years, we found we had so much more important things to talk about. I was blessed to have met him. I hope it's the same for you and Clint. He needs someone to care about him as much as you need someone to care about you."

"Thank you. I needed to hear that. Before Mom went to Iowa, I told her I wanted to have a chance to study history with you. At the time I didn't know you were living on the ranch."

"Since the class I teach to Chris, Mark and Peter corresponds with your early morning classes with Ken, Jerry and Dennis, it's not possible for you to monitor their classes. Hopefully, we can arrange to meet one or two days a week after our morning classes. I don't think Aaron will have a problem taking care of our son longer than usual."

"I don't want to be an imposition, but I would appreciate meeting with you. From what I've read, my historical education is lacking. I want to know what things were like before the aliens came to save our world. I also want to know if what I read in the historical romance novels is correct."

Caroline smiled. "You sound like some of the others I've met since I woke up, fifty years later than I ever expected. I was horrified when I learned how much of our world's history had been completely erased. I can hardly wait to start our meetings. I'll be in contact with you once Aaron and I work out our schedules."

The older woman went into the Complex, leaving Josie alone to enjoy the last of the September evening, watching the sun set behind the mountains.

This is all so different from Iowa. If I'm dreaming, please don't wake me up," she thought as she made her way up to her apartment.

Chapter Six

After going out to brunch with Ellie and Mike, Patsy waited with her friends for her flight to Nevada to be called.

"I don't want you to leave," Ellie said for the third time this morning.

"You know I can't stay here. Even for the short while I was home, I heard the rumors and the whispers when I was on the street. Starting a new life is for the best. I should have left Vern years ago and you know it. It's not like I'm going to be living on the moon. We'll be able to stay in touch through our communicators. Hopefully, you and Mike will be able to come down visit the ranch on your next vacation. I think you'll be impressed. I know I was when we first arrived."

"What about the trial for Vern?"

"I'm not sure there will be a trial, at least not in the foreseeable future. Cassion told me Vern has been transferred to a hospital for a criminally insane patient. His doctors seem to think his breakdown left him unable to assist in his own defense. I've seen this coming on ever since Jake went missing. I tried to get him to seek help, but he wouldn't listen. Look at where it got him. An innocent young man, who was Jake's friend, is dead, several others are wounded and he will never be a free man again. I have just sold everything he worked for. The life he worked so hard to build is completely gone. He has nothing, not even his family, to return to."

"Oh, Patsy, I know this has been hard for you. Mike and I are here for you whenever you need us."

Before Ellie or Mike could say more, Patsy's flight was called. With one last hug and a heartfelt good-bye, she made her way to the boarding area.

As she settled into her seat, the enormity of everything that transpired during her trip to Iowa came to the forefront. For the first time, in far too long, she felt as though she was in control of her life and her future.

~ * ~

Although Josie had her pilot's license, she still asked for someone to explain the controls of the hover craft she'd been assigned. While her father always traded vehicles every two years, he'd insisted she didn't need a new craft. The one she learned on was several years old and didn't have all the bells and whistles as her father called them.

"Are you sure you know how to fly this thing?" Clint asked.

"I do, but I need to know what everything does. The craft I flew at home was a much older model. I know what I'm doing, I just don't want to push the wrong button."

Clint laughed at her precautions, but she didn't let it bother her. She felt better knowing what everything on the craft did.

Once they lifted off, Clint ceased his teasing. If she didn't know better, she'd think he was afraid of flying. "You can let go of your armrest," she finally commented.

"I'm a lot more comfortable on the back of a horse. I can only remember flying in a hover craft two other times."

"Only twice?"

"Once when I was taken to Mexico by Grainger and again when I came here with Roger and Parker. I can't count the flight when I was rescued. I was probably too out of it to remember."

"I'm sorry I said anything. I tend to forget all the things you were denied. I was so anxious to start training for my pilot's license, my friend Kaye and I took her father's craft out one night before we were old enough to even start our training. We got caught, of course. I thought my dad was going to blow a gasket. I was grounded for a month and he wouldn't let me get my license until after I graduated from high school."

"What do you mean grounded?"

She felt foolish explaining the punishment she'd received when she knew he'd suffered throughout his life. "I was allowed to go to school, but that was it. I couldn't go out with my friends and I couldn't use my communicator for anything other than schoolwork. My dad kept it under lock and key and monitored every keystroke I made."

"Doesn't sound too bad to me, but maybe if I'd grown up like you did, I'd feel differently. I didn't even know what a communicator was until I got to Mexico City."

"I'm sorry. I'm certain you would consider my life to be one of privilege even though I see it differently. My dad wanted everyone to believe we had the perfect life. At home he blamed my mother for not watching Jake more closely. He blamed Zander for not wanting to play with the little kids at that picnic. Lastly, he blamed me for being a baby who needed my mother's attention. He never came to grips with what happened. He let his hate fester until it was ready to explode. The day we learned that Jake died when he was fifteen, he flew into a rage. He said he hoped Zander and I were happy that Jake would never become an adult. It was a terrible way to grow up We weren't physically punished for something we did wrong. We were emotionally abused for something that wasn't our fault."

"I never thought of things that way. It's hard for me to imagine what my life would have been like if I'd grown up with a family. Hopefully, we can help each other heal from the childhoods we endured."

Josie merely nodded her head in response. Below them the Las Vegas skyline came into view. After docking the craft, they went to the reception area where they would be meeting her mother.

~ * ~

Patsy prepared for the docking of the commercial hover craft. She thought of the recipe she carried with her from Lynette Warren. She'd contacted Mike to get the recipe to Cassion because as she said, he enjoyed her pecan pie so much during his visit. Thinking of the recipe made her smile, she was certain Cassion would be surprised when she brought it to him.

After they docked, she prepared to disembark and make her way to the reception area. Other passengers were leaving the craft ahead of her and she followed them to the reception area where she intended to meet

Cassion.

She was surprised to see Josie and Clint waiting for her. "I thought Cassion would be here," she said after they exchanged warm greetings.

"He had a lead on Foster Warren," Josie replied. "He left for Indiana early this morning. It was his suggestion that Clint and I come to meet your flight and take you back to the ranch."

"Who piloted the hover craft?"

"I did, Mom. It's not like I don't know how to pilot one. I have to admit it was much nicer than the one I had back in Iowa. Were you able to sell it?"

"Not yet, but all of our hover crafts as well as the furniture we weren't keeping are at the auction house. Mike is taking care of everything. I don't know what I would have done without him. He was able to find a buyer for the house as well as for the business. In other words, we have no legal ties to Iowa. It was hard enough being there to dispose of everything, with all the rumors and whispered accusations that were going on about your father."

Patsy could see tears forming in her daughter's eyes. Leaving the only home, she'd ever known, had been hard on her as well. At least she could go back to visit, while Zander would be confined to Resurrection Ranch for his part in Vern's plan to destroy what was being rebuilt here. It wouldn't be a life sentence, but the term he needed to serve would be evaluated on a yearly basis. She prayed that the people who were in charge would see he was swayed by his father's warped hatred that he'd grown up hearing.

~ * ~

Cassion landed at the Indianapolis hover port. He was lucky to be able to get a direct flight. As soon as he disembarked, he was met by one of his counterparts from the Indianapolis Complex. He'd met Zor on a couple of occasions and was glad to have someone he knew to depend on in finding Foster Warren.

"Have you been able to get any more information on our suspect?" he asked Zor.

"Not much. It seems he has no permanent address. He's been what they used to call 'couch surfing'. You know staying with friends until he wears out his welcome. The last address we have for him is in what they call shanty town several miles south of the city. He's been under surveillance ever since we received your request to find him. One of our agents got a line on him from someone in one of the homes where he was staying."

"How is that possible? We haven't made anything public."

"It was nothing less than a lucky coincidence. This woman, Anne Hoffman, came to the local police headquarters and told them her husband brought this guy home to spend a few days with them until he could get back on his feet. She said she didn't feel right about him and insisted her husband kick him out after three days. The last she knew her husband was taking the guy, Foster Warren, to shanty town. He's been under surveillance by our office ever since. Of course, if we hadn't had your bulletin on him and alerted the local authorities, none of this would have come to fruition."

"Thank the One God for looking out for us. I know I didn't put much in the bulletin about what he was wanted for. It was best if not many people knew what was going on. I have a picture of this guy with me. I hesitated on sending it over the communicators, because I've heard about how certain people are hacking into them. He's one of the men who have been kidnapping kids to take them to Henderson Ranch. We know he's been actively doing this within the past five years."

"I've been keeping up on the accusations against the Hendersons, as well as several other people connected to that hell hole. Let me see that picture."

Cassion, reached into his case and pulled out the picture Fredrick Wallace gave him less than a week earlier.

"That's him, for sure. How do you want to handle this?"

"We'll need to get the local authorities involved. I don't know about you, but I don't have the authority to arrest him."

"You're right. We're only here as advisors. I have a good relationship with the Chief of Police, as well as the county sheriff. Since shanty town is outside the city limits, we've involved the county officers to help us in the surveillance."

By the time they arrived at the Indianapolis Complex, officers from both the city and the county were waiting for them.

Once again, Cassion filled them in on the charges against Foster Warren and the importance of secrecy. There were to be no alerts put out over the radio. This had to be taken care of swiftly and privately.

~ * ~

Foster Warren was angry. He thought the guy he met in the bar a few nights ago would be his meal ticket for the next several days, if not weeks. That dumb bitch of a wife of his blew a gasket and told him, if he didn't get Foster out of the house, she was going to call the police to have him taken out bodily.

He wondered how he ended up in shanty town, rather on the comfortable couch at Pete Hoffman's house. Somehow, he was going to have to get even with her. If things were like they were a couple of years ago, he would have taken her kid and sold him to Henderson. Of course, that wasn't possible anymore. Damn that kid who turned Henderson in. Since that happened, he lost his steady income. In the past few years, he'd gotten Henderson to pay him fifteen thousand dollars for every kid he brought out there. It was a sweet ride for him.

He didn't have to work his ass off and he had enough money to put up a good front, no matter what state he was working in. He certainly wasn't like his twin brother. Fredrick thought he was so superior. He always held it over his head, with his fancy education and high paying job. He had to work five days a week, like the sheep going to slaughter. He didn't have to clock in and out and he lived the way he wanted to live. If he thought the accident that put his brother in a wheelchair would take him down a peg, he was completely mistaken.

After his pipeline to Henderson dried up, he was scratching for everything he got. His brother, on the other hand, was living high on the hog in Iowa. Life just wasn't fair.

He'd found am abandoned shack where he could stay and there was a soup kitchen that took care of the meals for those who lived in shanty town. They were pretty much all in the same boat, no money, no prospects, no food. At least he got two good meals a day.

Recently, he'd made friends with several of the other residents. Unlike him, most of them were hiding out from the law. Hell, the only thing he'd ever done was save boys from their mothers who were dirty whores or who were in foster care. Nobody gave two hoots about them, and for him it was a steady stream of income.

Thinking about Henderson Ranch, he remembered all the good times he'd shared with his twin brother, Noah Hammer, Delos Reynolds, and Theo Henderson. His brother was so different from the rest of his friends. He had more brains than a sense of adventure. As he recalled Fredrick always had his nose in a book and never wanted to go horseback riding with them.

Once his twin went to college, they went their separate ways. It didn't help that Fredrick lorded his education and top position with his company over him. He was actually happy when he learned about the accident at his brother's workplace. He thought it would take him down a peg, but he'd been sadly mistaken. That man could fall into a pile of shit and come out smelling like a rose.

It wasn't the same for him, He'd been scratching out a living for the last few years and finally hit rock bottom.

Outside of his shack, he heard a commotion. It was probably possible one of the derelicts who lived in the godforsaken place was being arrested. He was shocked when armed officers broke in his door.

"Foster Warren, you are under arrest," one of the officers shouted.

"You've got the wrong person," he protested. "I'm Fredrick Warren, you must be looking for my twin brother."

To his surprise, one of the aliens entered the room. "We have exactly the man we are looking for. I've met with Fredrick Warren and you resemble the picture he gave me of you."

"Who are you?"

"I am Cassion, from the Council of Intergalactic Affairs. You are under arrest for the kidnapping of young boys and selling them to Theodore Henderson. It is in your best interests to come with us willingly."

"I didn't do anything illegal," Foster protested. "Those kids were much better off on Henderson Ranch than they were living with whores or in foster care."

He knew it was a lie, but it was the best one he could think of at the moment. No matter how well treated he'd been growing up on that ranch, he knew Theo ran an entirely different operation once he inherited the property. If having the boys there wasn't profitable, he wouldn't have been able to pay the bounty he put on each of the boys.

"Where are you taking me?" he asked, once they put electronic cuffs on him.

"For now, you are being transferred to the Indianapolis Complex to await trial. You will be put in a secure cell and held without bail."

"Who are you to decide this? You're not a judge. I'm intitled to legal representation and…"

"…and you will be afforded that. I am a lawyer and I will be representing the Council in this matter. Because of your heinous crimes, I will be recommending you be held without bond."

"Heinous crimes, my ass. I was saving those kids. I grew up on Henderson Ranch and I turned out alright."

"That's your opinion. I've seen for myself the horrors of what was going on out there. I've also heard all about what the conditions were like and how the kids were sold to skinhead groups and ranches in Mexico as slave labor. Seeing grown men who were little more than walking skeletons and younger children with learning disabilities because of the treatment they received was enough for me to want to see anyone who perpetuated this abuse put away for the remainder of their natural life."

Foster knew he was caught. He couldn't talk his way out of this one. Even though he rarely took kids from healthy homes, he did look for any opportunity to grab a kid and sell him to Theo.

"I-I wasn't the only one."

"We know. Unfortunately, Delos Reynolds was murdered before he could be brought to judgement."

"What about Noah?"

"We haven't found him, but we will, it's only a matter of time. For now, I'm pleased to finally have located you."

~ * ~

Cassion couldn't believe how draining the capture of Foster Warren was. He realized, he'd been running on nervous energy ever since he got the lead on Franklin Warren and made the hurried trip to Iowa to check out the lead that gave him information on the man they now had in custody.

More than anything else, he wanted to get the first flight back to Resurrection Ranch. He needed to be with Hodia and if nothing else, consult with Dr. Gratan about the strange sensations he was experiencing.

"Are you alright?" Zor asked, as they watched Foster being taken to the police hovercraft to be transported to the Indianapolis Complex to be put into the secure custody of their own personnel.

These men were better prepared to handle hardened criminals like the man who, just minutes earlier, had been captured.

Unable to put voice to his feelings, Cassion could feel a weakness he'd never encountered before. Without uttering a word, he allowed the warm darkness of unconsciousness overtake him.

~ * ~

Zor was horrified to see his friend collapse before his eyes. He immediately called for an air ambulance. Luckily, one had been dispatched to go with them, in case open hostilities broke out.

Paramedics were immediately in the shack, pushing Zor out of the way. He never felt so useless in his entire life. He and Cassion had been friends growing up and came to Earth together from the dark side of the moon. Even though they were dispatched to the different complexes several miles away from each other, they'd kept in contact on a monthly if not weekly basis.

He'd followed the case that Cassion had been so engrossed in from the very beginning of the rescues and arrests. Deep in his heart, he envied his friend, until he saw how draining all of this had been for him. He was doing important work, while Zor spent long hours doing little more than paperwork. He hoped the trial for Warren would be held at his complex, so he could help Cassion with the prosecution of this monster.

"Can you hear us sir?"

Zor returned his attention to Cassion. Without verbal conformation, he nodded his head.

"Where should we transport him?"

Zor realized they were talking to him. "To the Indianapolis Complex. I'll call ahead and alert the medical facility that you will be bringing him in. I'll meet you there."

He watched as the paramedics put Cassion on a gurney and wheeled him to the waiting air ambulance. Before going to his hover craft, he contacted the complex.

"This is Zor. There is an air ambulance bringing in Cassion from shanty town. Please alert the medical facility to be ready for him. He collapsed."

"Do you know what is wrong with him?"

"I don't know. I fear it might be something serious."

After breaking the connection, he thought about his friend's condition. He'd seen Earthlings collapse and knew they were suffering from either malnutrition or stress. Things were different for people like Cassion. Their physiology was entirely different. He would have to get to the hospital and put his friend's life in the hands of the doctors.

~ * ~

Cassion could hear the paramedics talking to him, but for some reason, he couldn't give them a verbal answer. Listening to them, was like straining to hear what people were saying in another room. He had no idea what happened to him, but was relieved to know there were trained personnel taking care of him.

He heard Zor tell them to take him to the complex. He knew the doctors there would be able to assess his condition.

All through the ride, he thought about Hodia and wished Dr.

Gratan would be the one taking care of him. He didn't know the medical personnel at this complex and they didn't know him. He hoped they were on a par with Dr. Gratan.

Chapter Seven

Hodia couldn't help the feeling of dread that filled her all day. Something was wrong, terribly wrong, but she didn't know what it was. No matter how she felt, she still had duties at the educational center.

Early this morning, she monitored Josie's first solo teaching assignment with the older men who were attending the morning classes. She was pleased with how she handled each of their educational needs. They were the ones who tested ready for the secondary school level.

She knew this was going to be the most challenging of the classes she was being called upon to teach. Her students included Mark, Peter, Ken, Dennis and Jerry. With the educational opportunities available at the Denver Complex, Mark and Peter progressed with amazing speed. The others lived in one of the skinhead groups far longer than any of the others who had been rescued from either the skinheads or one of the slave ranches in Mexico. Somewhere along the line they had been given some education and added more once they left the group for a life of freedom.

The afternoon class was now down to two students rather than the original three. With the murder of Roger Blount, the demographic changed. She knew it was hard for Clint and Parker to attend the classes without their friend. Still, they came to class every day and were eager to be learning the things they missed learning as children. Both of them tested out at the seventh-grade level. That fact was surprising as they'd only begun their educational journey at the Mexico City Complex. It wouldn't be long before they were ready for the advanced education being provided to the other former residents of Henderson Ranch.

Hodia was preparing to go in to monitor the afternoon session, when Dr. Gratan stopped her.

"I thought I'd find you here," he greeted her.

"Is something wrong? I don't like the look on your face."

"It's Cassion. He was in on the take down of Foster Warren

and…"

"Was he injured?" she interrupted.

"Not in the way you're thinking. After the capture was complete, he collapsed. I had word from the Indianapolis Complex. I was asked to come out there to evaluate his situation. I was hoping you would be willing to accompany me. We can take the air ambulance as the doctors there think it would be best if he was cared for here. It's a blessing that Kara's parents are still at the ranch. They can take over for me at the hospital. Can you be ready to leave in say a half an hour?"

"Of course, I can. What do they think is wrong?"

"They're not certain, but they think it's associated with the stress he's been under ever since all of this began. I was told he's very weak and they are keeping him sedated."

Although she wanted to cry, Hodia held her emptions at bay. She had to be the strong one, the rock for her husband to cling to until he was back to his normal self.

"I'll meet you at the docking station in thirty minutes. I have to tell Chris and Melian where I'm going and have them take over my duties."

Dr. Gratan nodded his head in agreement and left to make his preparations for the flight they would be taking to Indianapolis.

Luckily, she found Melian and Chris in his office. They were as shocked as she was when they heard the news about Cassion's collapse.

Once she was assured, they would alert Mark to the situation at hand, she hurried to the apartment in order to pack an overnight bag for the trip she would be making with Dr. Gratan.

~ * ~

Chris was horrified to hear the news about Cassion. He'd been there for each and every one of the men who were rescued over the past several months. The man was nothing short of a rock for all of them. How could he have collapsed and be bad enough for Dr. Gratan and Hodia to be going to Indiana to be with him?

"You'd better go over to the office and alert Mark to what's going on. This is going to be hard, because he's always considered Cassion to be his mentor," Melian advised.

"I know. I'm just in a state of shock. He's been there for each and every one of us. What if…?"

"We can't think that way. From what Hodia said, they want to send him back here so he can get the rest he needs. I'll finish up here and you go over to see Mark. I'll meet both of you at the dining hall. We'll all have to put our heads together to decide how to handle things with him out of commission for a while."

She kissed him before leaving the office.

Taking a deep breath, Chris got up and left his office to walk across the door yard to tell Mark about these new complications. In his mind's eye the only thing he could think about was what would be the next disaster they would have to face.

He was pleased to see lights on in Mark's office. At least he wouldn't have to confront his friend in the dining hall where others might overhear what they were talking about, at least not until they decided how to broach the subject and tell everyone what was going on.

"Have you got a minute to talk to me?" Chris asked, as soon as he entered the office.

"You know I always have time for you. What's up?"

"Hodia and Dr. Gratan took the air ambulance to Indiana to pick up Cassion."

"Cassion? What wrong? Were they able to capture Warren? Was there…?"

"Slow down. There wasn't a scene like the one here a few weeks ago. Cassion collapsed after they captured Warren. They have him sedated but they feel he would be better off here. Dr. Gratan told Hodia his contemporaries at the hospital at the Indianapolis Complex think it's stress related and have sedated him until Dr. Gratan can get there."

It took a moment for Mark to respond. "We have to let the others know. Cassion has been such an influence to all of us, we have to make a plan for how we are going to continue on while he recuperates. Thank goodness Jason Culver got here last week. I know he's not a lawyer but he is familiar with the law."

"Now that you mention the law, I do think that Felton, Dan's mentor, is a lawyer. He's not the caliber of Cassion, but he does know the law. Hopefully, he can fill the gap until things get back to normal."

By the time they left the office, they'd devised a plan not only for informing the residents of Resurrection Ranch of what was going on, but also how they would be able to keep things running smoothly after this newest setback.

~ * ~

Josie was surprised when Hodia didn't come to the classroom to monitor her progress. When at last her class was over, Clint asked if he could accompany her to the dining hall.

She was pleased with his invitation. The picnic they'd shared just a matter of days ago awakened a feeling within her, she'd never experienced previously.

Once they arrived at the dining hall, the usual casual banter seemed to take on a more somber atmosphere. The chatter Josie expected to hear, was more like hushed whispers.

"What's going on?" Clint asked, as soon as Peter approached them.

"Your guess is as good as mine. I just got a message from Chris that he and Mark had an announcement to make. It's best if we get our food and find a table. Something tells me this announcement is best heard on a full stomach."

They no more than sat down at a table with Peter's mentor, Radon, than Mark and Chris entered the room. Even the hushed conversations ceased as though everyone anticipated the worst.

"We have an announcement," Mark began. "We got word today that Cassion collapsed and is in the hospital at the Indianapolis Complex. Dr. Gratan and Hodia left this afternoon to bring him back here for recuperation."

"That said," Chris added. "We all know that Cassion has been the glue that has been holding all of us as well as Resurrection Ranch together. In the meantime, we've talked to Felton and he's going to take over the legalities of running the ranch. He has his law degree and following the procedures Cassion has set in place should be relatively easy for him. Now that Jason Culver has taken over the position of security office, they should be able to handle anything that might come up."

"What's wrong with Cassion?" Parker asked.

"The only thing we know is that he collapsed. The doctors in Indianapolis have him sedated. They think it's stress, but they haven't run the tests that we can here. Dr. Gratan took the air ambulance and is planning to return here with him tomorrow or maybe the next day. After that, I'm certain he will be admitted to the hospital and will be resting once all the tests are finished. We've weathered a lot of storms in our lives and since we've returned to this ranch. We'll weather this one as well. The programs we have in place are all running smoothly and they will continue to do so, no matter what happens when Cassion returns. It's possible he might have to take a lesser role in the running of the ranch. It will be hard for him to step back and let the rest of us take on the lion's share of what he's been doing. Something tells me, he won't be receptive to stepping back a bit but we'll all make certain he gets the rest he needs."

Around the room conversation buzzed. Josie realized Cassion touched each of their lives in a different way. For her as well as her mother, he had been a life saver. He and Hodia accepted them and were helping them to acclimate to this new life. He had also been instrumental in helping Zander find redemption and gave him a new path to follow. She could only believe he'd done the same for many, if not all of the people who lived and worked here.

~ * ~

Even though Hodia knew their flight to Indianapolis wasn't a long one, it was to her. Cassion was hospitalized and she needed to be by his side. Every minute they were in the air, was more time away from the man she loved above all others.

Finally, the pilot announced they would be docking at the Indianapolis Complex within the next ten minutes.

She was surprised when Dr. Gratan opted to take a nap for the duration of the flight. It was possible he understood, once they landed, he would be too busy to rest. She knew once they were on their way back to Resurrection Ranch, he would get no rest because Cassion would be his responsibility alone. Since she had no medical education, the only help she could give would be supporting her husband and praying to the One God for strength and healing.

As soon as they docked, one of the doctors from the medical facility met them.

"What can you tell me about Cassion's condition?" Dr. Gratan asked.

"Is it all right to talk in front of 'her'?" the doctor questioned, nodding his head toward Hodia.

"I am his wife," Hodia replied through clenched teeth. "You can talk in front of me."

"We have kept him sedated. As you are well aware our physiology differs from that of the Earthlings. From what we can ascertain, he has been under great stress. He needs rest and lots of it. I'm afraid if he continues at the pace, he has been going I fear he will do unrepairable damage to his heart. We haven't been able to do many of the tests necessary in the short time he's been here. Since you brought an air ambulance, it looks like you are prepared to take him back to your facility for further treatment."

"That is our plan. For tonight, I would appreciate it if you would be able to find accommodations for Hodia. It's been a trying day for her and she needs to rest before we go back to Resurrection Ranch tomorrow."

"Resurrection Ranch? I've read about what you're doing out there. Are you certain you have the necessary equipment for the tests that need to be done?"

"Rest assured; we have a state-of-the-art medical facility. We have a fantastic group of backers and they have equipped us with everything we will ever need. I brought my own body scanner with me so that I can begin to ascertain what caused his collapse. Now, if you will take us to the room where he is staying, we will be more than grateful."

Hodia could tell the doctor who met them was far from impressed with the idea of them returning to Resurrection Ranch less than twenty-four hours after their arrival. She didn't like his attitude or his assumption that the home she now loved was little more than a backwater wide spot in the road. The sooner she could get Cassion home the better she would feel. She didn't miss the look on the man's face when Dr. Gratan mentioned his own body scanner. He looked as though he'd never heard of such a thing.

Cassion was sleeping peacefully when she entered his room. She wanted to take him in her arms and tell him how much she loved him. She also knew enough to keep her distance while Dr. Gratan did his initial examination with the body scanner. From the expression on his face, she knew the results were less than favorable.

"You called the instrument you used a body scanner. I have never seen one of those," the doctor who met them at the docking station said.

"This is a new invention, brought to me by my sister and her husband from the dark side of the moon. As you well know, the medical facilities there are the highest ranked in the galaxy. They are making great strides in medicine every day."

"I don't know if I trust instruments that have not been proven. What did your examination reveal?"

"Your initial diagnosis is correct. Cassion is suffering from stress. You were right to insist we come here. By tomorrow night, we will be back at the ranch where we can make a long-range plan for his treatment."

Hodia knew there was more to the diagnosis than what Dr. Gratan was saying. The doctor at this facility was definitely not used to people using the most up to date equipment. Just from looking at the man she was certain he came from beneath the ice cap of Antarctica. Where the people from the dark side of the moon were known for their medical ability, the people from Antarctica were known for education. She knew there were good doctors from there, but they did none of the research that had been done on the moon.

Chapter Eight

The next morning, they checked Cassion out of the hospital at the Indianapolis Complex and began the flight back to the ranch.

"Exactly what did the scanner say about Cassion's condition?" Hodia asked once they were airborne.

"The doctor at the hospital was right to diagnose stress as the reason for the collapse. What he didn't detect was the damage that has been done to Cassion's heart. We have been friends ever since we were children. If my findings are correct, he's in need of an emergency heart transplant. Luckily, Petro is one of the best heart surgeons available. He's also done extensive research on the artificial heart. A few days ago, he showed me the model he brought with him. I'm very impressed with it and it's exactly what Cassion needs. Last night, I contacted Petro and he is prepared to do the necessary surgery as soon as we land and get Cassion to the hospital."

Hodia couldn't hold back the tears she wanted to shed ever since they docked in Indianapolis. "Is it really that bad?"

"Unfortunately, it is. As you know, our lives either on the dark side of the moon or under the ice cap are relatively stress free. When the surgery is finished, I want to do a complete scan on you as well. Both you and Cassion have been under more stress than either of you are used to ever since Carolyn was miraculously brought back to life after one hundred years. First it was bringing her to Denver but that was only the tip of the iceberg. With each of the lost boys who were found the two of you have given one hundred and twenty percent to them. I should have been more observant. If I had been, I would have seen at least one of the warning signs."

Hodia's knees seemed to weaken enough that she moved to the side of the cabin of the ambulance and sat down on one of the seats. She questioned if there had been warning signs that she and Cassion missed.

She remembered the sleep times when Cassion was restless and unable to give in to his need for sleep. There had also been times when she'd been so exhausted, she'd gone back to their apartment rather than eat the noon meal, because she felt as though she needed a power nap before tackling her afternoon duties at the educational center.

"Can you do a scan on me, while we're traveling back to the ranch?" she finally asked.

"You know I can. Are you certain you want to know what I find before we dock?"

She nodded. "I want to know what I'm dealing with. I understand that Cassion has a severe problem. I need to be there for him, but at the same time I have to take care of myself. Am I making any sense?"

Dr. Gratan agreed.

Once she was lying on the second gurney, he prepared to run the scan. Not wanting to read anything into the expression on his face, she closed her eyes. She knew there would be no pain involved in the scan, but still she steeled herself for the exam to be over with.

"I'm finished, you can open your eyes."

"What did you find?"

"You have some minor damage. We've caught it early enough that everything can be controlled with medication and rest. In time it can be reversed if you do as you're told."

"What about the educational facility?"

"Where that's concerned, you will have to cut back on the hours you spend there. You have good teachers under you and I would recommend asking Carolyn to share part of the load with you. I have been in contact with Denver and they have another teacher who would be willing to relocate to assist with your facility. I have also been talking with Petro and Vernal and they have made the decision to stay on at the ranch. I can use the help at the hospital from Petro and Vernal is a trained nurse. She will be able to be with you as you regain your strength as well as care for Cassion after his surgery."

Hodia smiled for the first time since they started this trip. She was pleased to meet Petro and Vernal when they came to witness their daughter's marriage to Mark. She and Vernal formed an immediate friendship. It didn't come as a surprise to realize they'd decided to stay, since Mark and Kara were expecting their first child. What woman would not want to be involved the life of their first grandchild?

"Who is coming from Denver?"

"I think you will be pleased to think that your friend Astra will be joining us."

Dr. Gratan was right. She and Astra had been childhood friends. They'd even roomed together when they were studying to become teachers once they finished their secondary education. Together they would make a dynamic team.

~ * ~

The ranch was a beehive of activity. Dr. Petro didn't hesitate to step into the position Dr. Gratan left vacant when he went to bring Cassion home for treatment. Until he received the transmission from Gratan, he'd had very few demands made on his time. Now, he was preparing the hospital to perform the heart transplant he perfected with the synthetic heart in his clinic on the dark side of the moon.

As much as he would have liked to have his daughter, Kara, assist with the surgery, he knew she wasn't experienced enough for the job. Instead, he turned to Cindy Manning Amundson to stand by his side during the surgery. As soon as he met her, he was taken with her credentials as well as her ability to adapt to any medical situation that might arise.

"What time are you expecting the ambulance to dock, Dr. Petro?" Cindy asked.

"The last transmission I had was that they are at least a half an hour out yet. I'm satisfied that everything is ready for the procedure. How do you feel about it?"

"I am honored that you chose me. Your wife is far more experienced and I look forward to the educational opportunity you've offered me."

"My wife has assisted me before, but she is also the best anastasis I know. I wouldn't trust anyone else to fill that position. This is a very difficult procedure and it hasn't been done on Earth before."

"In my training I learned about the heart replacements of the past using both pig's hearts and mechanical ones. What make this one so unique?"

"The synthetic heart that I perfected is much closer to the humanoid heart than any of the other substitutes were."

"How is it that you had one of these with you?"

"I was asked, by my superiors, to bring one with me. It was inevitable that there would be an opportunity for me to do the operation while I was here. I have made arrangements with Radon to have the procedure recorded and sent to all of our complexes as well as to the top medical schools around the world."

From the look on Cindy's face, he could tell she was in awe of what he just told her. If this heart transplant worked on Earth as it had on the moon, it could change the world of medicine forever. Radon was also going to record all of the process, including the recuperation to be sent along with the footage of the operation itself.

Dr. Petro's wrist communicator signaled the docking of the air ambulance from the Indianapolis Complex. The communication also said that orderlies had been dispatched to the docking station and they should be ready to begin the operation, immediately upon their arrival.

With all the precision he was used to in his office on the moon, Cassion was brought directly from the docking station to the surgical suite. As planned, the operation began within minutes of the docking of the air ambulance.

~ * ~

Mark and Kara waited nervously for the arrival of the air ambulance. Ever since they heard about Cassion's collapse, the mood of everyone at the ranch became somber. The word that Cassion needed an immediate heart transplant brought more fear into the hearts of everyone on the ranch.

"How successful is this surgery?" Mark asked.

"My father has had great success with it on the moon, but it has never been performed on Earth before. Things are different here. It is a procedure that has been perfected by my father and his colleagues. Both of my parents are adamant about the success of this procedure. I wish I would be allowed to assist, but I will have to be content to watch the recording of it. His team is in place and I have to be content to sit this one out."

Mark knew Kara was disappointed when her father didn't choose her to be on his team. He felt honored to think his aunt would be assisting his father-in-law for this landmark surgery.

The announcement of the arrival of the air ambulance, prompted all work on the ranch to come to a halt. There was no one who hadn't been touched by Cassion in one way or another. Even though it wasn't time for a meal to be served, everyone gathered in the dining hall.

Their table was crowded when Peter, Jerilyn, Chris and Melian joined them to wait for the outcome of the surgery.

"I was told that Hodia was also hospitalized and has to curtail many of her duties," Chris said.

Jerilyn nodded. "She has a lot of responsibility at the learning center. It was the same in Denver. I've known her longer than the rest of you. She's always gone above and beyond for everyone who needs her help. I've also been told that Astra will be arriving from Denver tomorrow to assist both Hodia and Carolyn in their duties."

"I remember her," Chris said. "I had her as a teacher for a few of my classes when I first arrived at the Denver Complex. You had her as well, didn't you Mark?"

"I did and she was an excellent teacher. I hope she will consider staying on permanently. We've put together a top team, but the two people who we depend on the most are now incapacitated. It's always good to have others on our team who can step in to keep things running smoothly."

"With all this talk about what's going on, do we know where Foster Warren will be tried?" Peter asked. "I know he's not the one who brought me here, but he's brought several others to the ranch. I think it's only right the trial should be held here."

"You forget we don't have a secure place to hold him," Mark

replied. "I talked to several of the other mentors about it and they are suggesting he be taken to the Nevada Complex for trial. His crimes were perpetuated for the profit of this ranch. It's only fitting he be brought here. The authorities here are in the process of filing the papers for his transfer."

Around the table there were several comments about the disposition of Foster Warren's trial. Although they all wanted to see justice done, many of them wanted the trial to be held at the ranch, rather than in Carson City. It seemed like a long way for any of them to travel to see justice done. Of course, they all knew there was still one man who was to be found before justice could be completed.

~ * ~

Minutes turned into hours as time seemed to drag. Although the evening meal was served, it seemed as though no one had the appetite to do it justice.

"I can't stand this suspense," Chris said. "When do you think we'll hear something?"

"I'm of the same opinion," Kara replied. "It's an extremely complicated operation. I talked to my father as well as my mother while we were waiting for the air ambulance to arrive. He told me it could take up to twelve hours to complete. We have to be patient, no matter how hard it is. This isn't something that can be rushed."

"We all understand the importance of your father taking his time," Melian said, joining the conversation. "It's just that Cassion and Hodia are so important to everyone on this ranch, we are all concerned."

As though on cue, Kara's communicator buzzed. When she answered it, she put it on speaker so everyone at the table could hear what her father had to say.

"As far as I'm concerned, the operation was a great success. The next few weeks will be crucial in his recovery, but I don't foresee any complications. As for Hodia, she is resting comfortably and not having any adverse reaction to the medications Dr. Gratan prescribed for her."

Before Kara could respond or her father could continue, there was a rousing cheer from everyone gathered in the dining hall.

As though the atmosphere changed instantly, everyone suddenly regained their appetite and the normal chatter replaced the subdued silence of only minutes earlier.

Chapter Nine

The following morning, Josie arrived for her early morning class and was greeted by Caroline Phillips.

"I'm pleased to see you here so early," Caroline greeted her. "I'm certain you've been told that Hodia has been hospitalized for, not only rest, but for her to become comfortable with the medication Dr. Gratan is giving her."

"Yes, I was in the dining hall when Dr. Petro contacted Kara. I can't believe the two most important people to Resurrection Ranch are in such dire condition."

"That's where you're sadly mistaken, my dear. Everyone on this ranch is important. It's true that Cassion and Hodia have been instrumental in the building process of not only this ranch, but also the educational facility. That said, the rest of us are going to be taking up the slack until Hodia's friend Astra can arrive from Denver. I had a message this morning saying she was being delayed and asking me if I could take over Hodia's duties until she can arrive. That means I would like you to take over my history classes for a while."

"Me? I'm afraid I don't know enough."

"You'll do just fine. I've written out a detailed lesson plan. There should be no problem with it. I checked your schedule and the history class for the oldest of the young men is an hour after your morning class. Everything is self-explanatory. I know you haven't had much contact with Ken, Dennis and Jerry, but you'll find them very receptive students."

Josie was astonished at Caroline's confidence in her abilities. "Thank you. I'll do my best. I do realize that at this time, we all have to do over and above. I know I was never abused, like the young men who are just now getting their educations, but I feel a strong attachment to not only the ranch, but everyone here."

"I knew I made the right decision when I decided to ask you to take over my class for a few days. You have more reasons to despise this ranch than anyone I know."

"You have me confused with my father. Unlike my brother, I didn't buy into his crap. He's been filled with hatred ever since Jake was kidnapped. If you listen to my father, Jake was the golden child. Zander and I were nothing more than bitter reminders of what he lost. I was lucky that I didn't have to listen to his hateful preaching. Zander couldn't get away from it because he worked closely with our father in his insurance office. I've felt nothing other than love and acceptance since I got here."

Caroline smiled broadly. "Even though the reason you came here was disastrous, I think you've found your calling here. As I know, you've caught the eye of a certain young man."

Josie blushed at Caroline's reference to Clint. He had, indeed, caught her eye as well. Unlike the boys her father insisted she date back home. He was down to earth and forth coming with any information about his past she was interested in hearing.

The buzzer rang, indicating it was time for the first classes for the day to begin. Taking a deep breath, we went into the classroom where she was scheduled to meet with Peter and Mark. At first, she'd questioned why Chris wasn't in her class, but she was assured he was taking his classes under Melian's watchful eye. It made sense, considering they were husband and wife. He was busy with the running of the educational facility. Their classes were held in the evening, when they returned to their apartment.

As usual, Mark and Peter turned in their homework assignments. Both of them took their classes very seriously.

Setting the homework aside, she began to layout the lesson plan for the day. This morning, they were studying geography, not only of the United States, but of the world, as it was now.

She wondered what the map of the United States looked like before the disaster of the mid twenty-first century obliterated much of the east and west coasts of this country.

On the current map, she distinguished each of the remaining states, as well as the countries of Europe, Africa, Australia, along with North and South America. She did a lot of planning for this particular lesson. Thankfully, she'd always enjoyed geography at each level of her education.

"I know you both have jobs to do, but your homework for tomorrow is to fill in as many names for the states as you can identify. I don't mark down for spelling, but this will give me a baseline for the amount of studying you will need to be able to identify them without a problem. Also, I would like to have you list the states and countries you can remember being in."

She fully expected to hear groans at the assignment, but they seemed to be excited about the assignment.

"I wish I could say I've been in several states," Mark said. "That's something I'd like to do."

"Why can't you?" she inquired.

"There's too much to do on the ranch."

"In time, perhaps you can do some traveling to promote the ranch. I'm certain there are other troubled young men who could rewrite their futures here. It's something to think about. I know Zander is grateful for the opportunity he has been given to turn his life around here."

"I hadn't thought about that," Mark replied. "It might not happen for several years, but two years ago I didn't think I would ever be free. Like Cassion has told me, anything is possible."

"It certainly is."

"How many different countries and states have you been in, Josie?" Peter asked.

Her lack of travel experience was suddenly embarrassing. "I've lived my entire life in Iowa. My father would never allow us to leave for any amount of time, since he was certain Jake would come home any day and when he did, he wanted to be there. I've seen the Mississippi River but very little else. When we came to the ranch, it was the first time I left my home state."

"When you first arrived, I envied you. You had a normal family life," Peter said. "I can see now that your life wasn't much different than ours. You were given an education, but you were as much of a prisoner as we were, only your captor was your father."

Josie could make no reply. Any words she would have wanted to speak were stopped by the tears that threatened to fall and the lump in her throat she couldn't swallow down. Pulling herself together, she dismissed the class early. She knew she needed time to prepare for the next class and come to grips with what Peter just told her.

She'd often thought of her life and even mentioned it to her mother, but for others to see the pain she'd lived through since Jake's disappearance came as a disturbing surprise. Resurrection Ranch was part of her life now just as it had been part of Jake's life when it was run by the Hendersons.

Rather than dwell on the past she realized she had to look forward to the future. Picking up the detailed lesson plan Caroline gave her; she went over the material. To her surprise, the lesson was based on the Civil War. A war that tore apart the country with north vs. south. Looking at the dates, she realized it took place over two hundred and fifty years earlier. The words about the slavery practiced in the south slapped her in the face. Even if the end of the war made slavery illegal, Clint told her about how he'd been branded by the man who bought him as a slave.

Unbidden tears flowed down her cheeks, as she thought about the men, women and children who had been held as property so many years earlier. The atrocities they suffered resurfaced to be experienced by the young men who had been returned to this ranch to erase the past and work for the future.

The sound of the buzzer predicated the arrival of the oldest of the lost boys. She hadn't officially met them, but she'd seen them across the dining hall. They intrigued her, since their lives, like Chris', had taken an entirely different path from the others who were sold to the slave ranches.

From what she could ascertain, the skin head groups inflicted a different type of torture. Along with not enough food, she learned there had been intense brainwashing and harsh military training.

It didn't seem to surprise the three men who entered the class room to find her as their teacher.

"Mrs. Caroline told us you were going to be our teacher," Jerry said, extending his hand. "We've been wanting to meet you. I'm Jerry, these are my friends, Dennis and Ken. We were all in the same skin head group. Ken was the first to leave and he prompted me to do the same. It took a while for us to convince Dennis to join us. We were luckier than many of the younger boys. We've been given the rudiments of education since we left the group."

"I'm pleased to meet all of you. I was reading over the lesson plan about the Civil War. I think this is the most important lesson I will ever present."

"I've been reading about it," Ken replied. "I've been out the longest and have been given the tools to look things up on my communicator. I've been reading the information that Mrs. Caroline unearthed. When I knew that would be today's lesson, I did some research. I thought the slavery of the ranches in Mexico as well as the skin head groups was made illegal, by the Emancipation Proclamation at the end of the Civil War. I wish I would have been able to testify at the trial for the Hendersons as well as the Grangers."

"We were all interested in this period," Dennis said. "Ken shared what he'd learned and we've had a lot of discussions about it. Did you know about it before today?"

"I'm sorry to say I didn't. It's one of the most incredible stories I've ever read. I think it is so relevant to everyone who grew up here and was sold, it should be taught to at least all of the older men. As for the youngsters, it is something that can wait until they are older, but it's imperative that they learn the past. I've heard that history repeats itself and if we don't learn from the past, we are bound to repeat it in the future. The fate of the young men who survived the treatment they received here in the past is living proof that this is true. Since you've done your pre-research on this topic, I think we would all benefit from a spirited discussion."

Throughout the hour, the three men commented on what they'd found on their communicators regarding this period in the history of the United States. She was surprised at how much they gleaned on their own, and enjoyed the discussion, more than she would have if she'd merely stuck with the lesson plan.

As soon as the class ended, she made her way to Hodia's office. Caroline was seated behind the desk working on the paperwork that would have normally been done by Hodia.

"How did your class go?" she asked.

"I read over the lesson plan and realized how relevant it is to this ranch. I was thrilled when Dennis told me he'd done research on this period on his communicator. We had quite a unique class period as we engaged in a good discussion. I was wondering if you would be receptive tutoring me in history. I am so interested in learning from the past. I also think my two classes with the younger men would benefit from this knowledge as well."

"I totally agree. The only problem is that they are still getting the skills to go onto higher learning. You're their teacher. Do you think they're advanced enough to understand the history of this country?"

"I most certainly do. It's amazing how advanced they are. I didn't know what to expect. This morning's lesson was geography. While they have limited exposure to such things, they are eager to learn. If nothing else, I think they should be taught about the Civil War. This is one subject they would completely understand considering the lives they have been leading. I know how much reading this lesson plan and the following discussion we participated in this morning affected me. I'm certain it will be the same for them."

"You are, indeed a gift from the One God. Even though I've known of their background since the first day I met Chris, I worried about exposing them to too much history before they were able to grasp the elementary education they were denied. When Astra arrives, let's plan to get together not only to plan a session with the middle group of students, but also to arrange a time for the two of us to set a time for your history lesson."

Josie was delighted. Never in her wildest imagination would she have thought her thoughts on the class schedule for her regular students would be accepted by anyone with Caroline Phillips' knowledge of the past.

~ * ~

Patsy Rawlins thoroughly enjoyed working in the dining hall with Conner and Julia. Their culinary skills were excellent and she was eager to learn anything they could teach her. She was skilled at making everyday meals for her family, but she soon realized she didn't have the expertise to use spices and herbs to bring out the most flavor in the food they served the residents of Resurrection Ranch.

She'd just finished the morning shift when Josie entered the dining hall. "I didn't expect you so early. Lunch won't be served for another two hours."

"I know, but I had to tell you about what happened to me today."

"It must be something important. I know that Clint is working, so it must not have anything to do with the two of you."

"It does and it doesn't. Caroline Phillips met me at the educational facility before my first class and asked me to take her class with the older men for a few days while she fills in for Hodia. After my regular class, I took the opportunity to talk to her privately. She's agreed to add history to the middle students and to tutor me. I'm so excited about this. I also got to meet the older students and they were very receptive to having me as their teacher today. I know they're all older than me, but we seemed to hit it off right away. To be truthful, I will be sorry to only be their substitute teacher, but I know Caroline will be able to meet their needs more so than I am."

Patsy reached across the table where they were sitting and took her daughter's hand in hers. "I know this is something you've wanted. You will learn a lot from her, just don't overextend yourself. Remember you have two classes that you're teaching every day plus you need to reserve time for Clint. I can see he's quite taken with you. As far as I'm concerned, he's a fine young man. Don't cheat him of time with you."

"I won't, I promise. This is an opportunity I've wanted to partake in ever since I first heard about the history, she was able to return to the people of our generation."

When Josie left the dining hall to return to their apartment, Patsy stayed seated at the table. While she was in Maquoketa, she questioned the move that she perceived as necessary. Now she saw this was the best decision she'd made. Josie was blossoming more than ever before in her life. She'd made certain her daughter had the best education she could afford, even over Vern's objections. Even at that time, she'd never seen the joy that radiated from Josie's eyes over the events of a few hours this morning.

Chapter Ten

Clint always looked forward to the end of the day. Not only did it mean he would be meeting with his friends in the dining hall, but also after the evening meal, he would be seeing Josie in their evening class. At times he wished it was just him and Josie in the classroom. It wasn't like he wanted to deny Parker the educational time. He only wanted more time with the woman who now dominated his every waking moment.

"Are you ready for our class tonight?" Parker asked.

"You know I am. I finished my homework after class last night."

"I know you did, that wasn't what I meant. It's evident you're taken with our new teacher. She is a lovely young woman. I'm happy for you. Maybe someday I'll meet someone who will be just as special to me."

"I've heard there are some new counselors and nurses coming from both the dark side of the moon and under the ice cap of Antarctica. Who knows, you might find someone special sooner than you think."

Parker playfully punched Clint in the arm. "Not unless we do the best we can do in class. Mrs. Hodia told me that by the end of the semester we will be able to move on to the secondary level. Once we finish our education, what do you think you want to do with the rest of your life?"

Clint thought over the question his friend posed. The future was something he hadn't contemplated before. He loved ranching, but he wanted more. What it was he wanted? He didn't know.

"I'm not sure. For most of our lives we've only lived from day to day. Right now, I can only think about one tomorrow at a time. What about you?"

"I'm happy doing ranch work, but once our education is ended, who knows what my decision will be. To be truthful, I'd like to teach ranching to young men who have led troubled lives. As far as I'm concerned, the best place to do something like that is right here. Since we've been rescued, I've heard there are troubled young men who need structure in their lives. We won't be ready to help them right away, but in a few years, it might be something we can institute."

Parker left their dorm room with Clint having more questions than answers about the future. He liked the idea Parker planted in his mind. Education and structure were two things that were missing in his life when he grew up here.

As usual, when he thought about the past, he rubbed the brand on his left arm. It was a constant reminder about the nightmare from which he'd been rescued. It was comforting that Josie accepted this visual reminder. It was entirely possible she had emotional reminders he would never be able to see.

~ * ~

Josie was still bubbling with excitement as she made her way to the dining hall. She knew she would see Clint. Rather than telling him about the opportunity Caroline offered her earlier in the day, she would concentrate on his day. Instead of eating with her brother she would seek Clint out. She knew he was embarrassed by his lack of education, even though that was the least of her worries where he was concerned.

"Hi Sis, how was your day?" Zander asked when she entered the dining hall.

"It was great, but…"

"I know you don't want your big brother cramping your style with a certain young man,"

"How did you know?"

"This is a small community. There isn't much that is kept secret for too long. To be truthful, I couldn't be happier. I've never seen you glow like this. I'm sorry for what Dad did to you, what I did to you. I bought into his opinions about this place. It was wrong. The more I work with these people the clearer things become for me. I still can't believe they can be so forgiving of me, for the things I did against them. I heard this morning that Dad is going to be committed to a facility for the criminally insane for the killing of Roger Blount. It's only fitting. He's been slipping into insanity for far too long. It's time for the punishment he deserves. Unfortunately, nothing can ever change what he did to our lives in the process."

Josie hugged her brother and for the first time in her life realized he did understand how their father shaped their lives. She thanked the One God that her father hadn't corrupted her mind to the same extent as he did Zander.

Zander left to find a table where he would sit for dinner. At that moment, Clint entered the dining hall.

"You look like the cat who swallowed the canary," he greeted her. "Did something special happen to you today that has you so excited?"

"Something did happen today, but I'd rather hear about your day."

"What's there to tell? I was punching cattle and thinking about you."

"I'm flattered. To be truthful, I was thinking about you today as well."

"Will you eat dinner with me?"

"I'd love to. Do you think Parker will join us? I want to get to know both of you better, only not as students."

"Maybe another time. He's decided that if you were willing to join me, he didn't want to be a third wheel, so to speak. Let's fill our plates and you can tell me all about what happened to you today."

Her best laid plans were suddenly derailed. She wondered how she could be so excited about her new educational opportunity when she knew he was still learning at an elementary level. Hopefully, that would change by the end of the semester when he and Parker would certainly be advanced to the secondary level where Peter and Mark were studying.

After filling their plates with roast beef, green beans, mashed potatoes and gravy, they found a table for two in a secluded corner.

"Okay, we have our meal, now it's time for you to spill the beans," Clint said, after holding out the chair for her. "I can tell there's something you're busting to tell me."

"Yes, there is, but I don't know how you'll feel about it. I've been offered the opportunity to study history with Caroline."

"Why would I feel anything but excitement for you? I've heard all about how she restored history when she was discovered at the archaeological dig in the California wastelands. I've talked to Peter and Mark about the classes they've been taking from her. They are so excited to learn about history, it makes me even more pumped to be able to move on to the secondary level of education. The only problem is will you still be my teacher?"

Josie could feel a blush creeping into her cheeks. "I hope by the end of the semester, I will have learned enough to continue on as your teacher. At that level, you will have several teachers, each concentrating on different areas of study. I'm certain I will be able to fill one of those positions for you and Parker."

"That's fine with me as long as the only time Parker shares you with me is in the classroom. Speaking of Parker, he brought up something I hadn't thought of before earlier. He mentioned he wanted to teach troubled youth to become ranchers and get some structure in their lives."

"What a marvelous idea. I'm certain that's something Mark, Chris and Peter will be interested in exploring. At least that's what Melian was telling me about the plans for the future of Resurrection Ranch the other day."

Before they could continue their conversation further, Jason Culver entered the dining hall. She'd met him briefly when he first came to the ranch to fill the position of law enforcement officer.

"I have an announcement to make," Jason said, silencing all of the conversations that dominated the room earlier.

"We have a line on where to find Noah Hammer. We have people from the Kansas City Complex, who are hoping to apprehend him within the next few days. Since Resurrection Ranch is an enmity unto itself, I want to propose holding the trials for both Noah and Foster here. I need to see what everyone thinks of the idea. If it isn't feasible, they will be held in Carson City, as were the trials for the Hendersons and the Grangers for their part in how this ranch was run. As far as I'm concerned, most of you have had your lives affected by these people and you should be able to see that their punishment will be swift. It's one thing to hear about these trials second hand and another to witness the process in person."

To Josie's surprise, Zander was the first person to get to his feet. "I didn't live through the nightmare like a lot of you. It was a man who was like these two destroyed my family, as well as my childhood and that of my sister. It is only right they should be able to see what damage their actions have done to everyone here."

Josie silently applauded her brother's decision to make the comment. Within a few moments, the room seemed to explode in not only conversation but applause. It made her proud to think that the man everyone here feared only a matter of weeks earlier, now put voice to what everyone else was thinking. Knowing the hatred their father preached for their entire lives, it was amazing at how things had changed for Zander since coming to this ranch.

"Bravo, Zander," she heard someone say.

Looking around the room, she saw Mark on his feet. One by one, every one of the lost boys joined him in standing and singing Zander's praises. Even Clint got to his feet, prompting her to do the same.

"I think Zander speaks for all of us," Chris said as the applause died down. "We all deserve to see justice meted out at the place where their actions did the most damage. I testified at the trial for the Hendersons as well as for the Grangers. Mark was able to face the Grangers at their trial and I know Peter faced his own demons when he testified against his father for sending him here through Delos Reynolds. These men changed our lives, and we all need to see justice done."

Josie turned to face Clint. From the look in his eyes, she knew one of the two men who were going to be tried for kidnapping and trafficking entered his life at an early age.

"Are you alright?" she asked, once they returned to their seats to continue their meal.

He didn't respond, nor did he continue eating. Instead, he pushed his food around on his plate, his eyes downcast.

"Are you…?"

"I hadn't heard the name of the second man who they were looking for before tonight," he interrupted. "Hearing the name of Noah Hammer brought back a bad memory. He was the grounds keeper at the foster home where I was living. I remember there were a lot of kids there.

One day, he told me we were going on a trip. I was only three but I still remember him taking me away from there and bringing me here. I've been trying to remember how I got here and once I heard his name it all came back to me."

Clint's eyes filled with moisture and she could tell he was remembering how he came to be brought to Henderson Ranch

Josie ached for Clint. The horrible memories he'd hidden so deeply, had to be terrifying to him. "I think it's best if rather than having class tonight, we talk about what Officer Culver just told us. I have a feeling the two of you might be able to tell a similar story about whoever it was who brought you here."

As though the words she spoke were exactly what they needed to hear, the cloud of uncertainty seemed to lift from their eyes.

"I think that's a good idea."

One by one, the lost boys, their mentors and those who cared about them began to gather around the table where Josie and Clint were sitting. Even Zander joined them.

It was Jerilyn who spoke first. "I know you have a class scheduled for tonight, but I think everyone needs to be together in order to come to the correct conclusion about these trials. I'm willing to offer my services to anyone who wants to join us."

Josie smiled. "Parker, Clint and I were just talking about the same thing. If you hadn't come over, Jerilyn, I would have sought you out. This is going to be another one of the healings that have been taking place here. I think we all can use your help."

~ * ~

Mark marveled at the outpouring of alliance from everyone who lived and worked on Resurrection Ranch. Over the past few weeks, he'd seen a marked change in Zander. For him to be the first to stand and say the words everyone was thinking took a lot of courage. He'd said it before, Zander and Josie were victims of the acts of men like Delos, Foster and Noah even though they'd never been taken from their parents.

"Are you planning to go to the meeting that Josie and Jerilyn are planning?" Kara asked.

"How can I not? We've all been affected by what those men did. I was sent here by the state, because I had no other place to go. At that time, they thought they were doing what was best. No one knew what was going on here until Chris was rescued and insisted more of us should be found. If I hadn't been rescued when I was, you know I would be dead now. You should, because it was you who nursed me back to health."

He watched as Kara put her hand over her still flat stomach. It was within the confines of her body where their child grew. By having the trials for the two kidnappers held here, it would send a chilling message to anyone who might, in the future, decide to perpetuate the horrors that transpired on this property.

~ * ~

To Josie's surprise, it didn't take long for the dining hall to be converted to a meeting place. She was pleased when the mentors joined her and Jerilyn at the front of the room.

With the names of the monsters who dominated the dreams of many of the young men who grew up here made known, this would be one of the most important meetings ever held on the ranch.

"With Officer Culver's announcement tonight, it is possible buried memories have come to the forefront for many of you," Jerilyn said, starting the meeting. "This is a time for everyone to say what they think of having the trial for these two men held here on the ranch."

Josie scanned the room. She could see clouded memories coming to the forefront for all of the young men she'd met. It was amazing to see many of the aliens and others who relocated to the ranch in attendance. Toward the back of the room, she saw Cassion and Hodia enter. Even though she knew they would want to be part of the meeting, she worried about how tonight's discussion would affect either of their recoveries. It came as a relief when Dr. Petro and his wife Vernal took their places behind the aliens who were the heart of the ranch.

It was Peter who next stood to speak. "I've made no secret that I was kidnapped by my father and brought here by his 'friend' Delos

Reynolds. It doesn't break my heart to know that Delos was murdered by my father. That said, I wish he was still alive in order to face the judgment that his friends, Foster and Noah will be given. I ask you now if anyone remembers their kidnapper. If so, do you want him to be brought to justice here on the ranch?"

For a moment, a hush fell over those who were assembled. To everyone's surprise, it was Brad who got to his feet.

"I remember living in a foster home, but I don't know why I was there. When I heard Officer Culver say the name of Noah Hammer, I remembered him. He worked at the home. One day he took me on an outing, but I didn't come back to the home. I came here. I didn't like living in the home, but I liked being here even less. I don't want to see him again, but I want to be able to help in the accusations against him."

Josie looked at Clint. Brad's story mirrored Clint's so closely, she wondered if they had been taken from the same foster home. Was it possible that the foster parents were as involved as the two men who would soon be going on trial?

One by one, others got to their feet and put voice to their stories. Of those who were working on the ranch where they'd grown up, the stories were all close to the same as the ones Brad and Clint told.

By the end of the discussion, a vote was taken. Not one person in attendance voted against having the trial held on Resurrection Ranch. It was now in the hands of the courts as to when and how a trial could be scheduled to be held on the ranch still haunted by the horrors perpetuated by the men who would soon be tried for their criminal acts.

As everyone was leaving the room, Josie sought out Peter's mentor, Radon. She was well aware that he was taking over many of the aspects of the duties Cassion was curtailing. Perhaps she would tell him of her assumptions about the foster homes from which Clint and Brad were kidnapped.

"Is there something I can help you with?" Radon asked.

"I don't know if there is anything to this but my vivid imagination," Josie began. "When Brad told his story, it was almost word for word like the story Clint told me just an hour earlier. Do you think the foster homes where they were living when they were kidnapped are in on this?"

Radon's eyes opened wide at her suggestion. "We need to talk to Cassion and Hodia about this."

His suggestion startled Josie. She prayed Cassion and Hodia were strong enough to be involved in the implication of the foster parents in the terrible crimes committed by Noah Hammer.

"Your concern is appreciated, but unnecessary," Cassion said. "Dr. Petro is right here and he tells me, even though I have to slow down, I'll be good as new in a couple of weeks. Your assumption has merit. In the morning, we will be contacting all of our complexes in the United States and Canada. It's time we looked into the homes from where Brad and Clint disappeared. It's possible we're only scraping the tip of the iceberg. I'll also be contacting the penal colony on the dark side of the moon for further interrogation of the Hendersons. One way or another we will get to the bottom of the atrocities perpetuated on this ranch. I assure you, once the calls are made, I will leave the investigation of this up to the others. I will not jeopardize my health again."

Josie was relieved. Returning to Clint's side, she told him of the conversation she'd had with Cassion and Radon about her suspicions. She also explained the things that would be happening over the next few days.

"Do you think Brad and I were both taken from the same foster home?" Clint asked.

"It's possible. You heard Brad's memory. It's almost word for word the same as yours. Even if the two of you were from different homes, it's possible everything was orchestrated by the Hendersons and Hammer. Where this ranch is concerned, nothing is absolute. We'll just have to wait and see how everything plays out."

~ * ~

Patsy listened intently to everything that was said at the meeting. Even though she had no comments to make, she knew she'd been as much of a victim as the young men gathered here tonight.

When she saw Josie talking to Cassion, she remembered his trip to Iowa while she was in the hospital. As she recalled, he'd made contact with Frederick Warren, the twin brother of the man who had been taken into custody prior to Cassion's collapse. Could it be possible he would ask Frederick Warren to return to Resurrection Ranch for the trial?

As though Cassion read her thoughts she saw him approaching her.

"I know you never got to meet Fredrick Warren, but I have a feeling you will be meeting him and his wife Lynnette in the near future. Once we have Hammer in custody and the trial set, I will be contacting them to come here to testify for the prosecution. I know it will be hard for him to testify against his twin brother but it's something that I must ask him to do."

"From what you've told me, his time at Henderson Ranch in no way resembled what it became in later years. Do you actually think he will agree to return here?"

"I hope so. Unlike the young men who returned here for an education and to build the ranch, he harbors none of the terrible memories."

Patsy nodded. Each of the young men she'd met here had stories of the abuse and forced labor they'd endured. Most of all, her mind went to Roger Blount, the young man who called her son Jake his friend and died at the hands of her deranged husband. She also thought of Parker Flint, Clint Anders, and Peter Sims-Hodges who all bore the brand of the master they'd been sold to by Mr. Henderson. Her mind went immediately to her son, Jake. Had he not died, she wondered if he would have been branded as a slave like his friends. It was entirely possible, but like Peter and the others told her, Jake was the lucky one. He never had to live as a slave, owned by a master with no regard for life.

"You're deep in thought," Cassion observed. "Would it be improper to ask you what's on your mind?"

"It wouldn't be improper. I was thinking about what this ranch became and Jake's three friends, who suffered much more than he did. Jake lost his life, but he never had to be sold into slavery as they were. They all told me, Jake was the lucky one. The more I learn about the young men who are working so hard to bring this ranch back to life, the more I agree with them."

"As much as it galls me to say this, I agree with you completely. The many boys who lost their lives on this ranch most certainly gained eternal life with the One God. I can also understand your husband's state of mind over the loss of his youngest son, although I don't condone his actions. As soon as the dates for trial are set, I will be certain you are advised about the status of Frederick Warren."

With that, Cassion returned to the table where he had been sitting with his wife earlier. It struck her at how frail he appeared. It was certainly too soon after his surgery, for him to be sitting here during this emotion packed discussion.

Chapter Eleven

Noah Hammer was shocked when he heard of Foster Warren's capture in Illinois. As soon as he'd heard about the raid on Henderson Ranch, he knew his source of additional income suddenly dried up. He immediately contacted Jasper Constantine.

Jasper was older than Noah, Foster, and Theodore. It was his idea of taking boys from the foster care system. He went to college after ageing out of the program that Theodore's father ran, and eventually was hired by a company who oversaw several foster homes.

After Delos, Foster and Noah aged out of the program, they stayed together for several years, pulling off petty crimes to survive, while working at low paying jobs. About five years after leaving Henderson Ranch, they'd been contacted by Jasper and Theodore. A meeting between the five of them was set up in Las Vegas.

At that meeting Jasper and Theodore laid out the plans for a scheme that would make them all rich. Jasper would target young boys from the foster homes, while Noah and Foster took the young boys and brought them to the ranch that Theodore now owned outright.

While Noah enjoyed working at the foster homes and spiriting away a young boy every couple of years, Foster as well as Delos didn't want to work for Jasper. They made their own contracts with Theodore, taking children whenever the opportunity presented itself.

Delos had been careless when he contracted with individuals who had kids they wanted to have disappear. On his last job, he had joined forces with a serial killer who didn't want to split the profits. It served him right. If he'd followed Jasper's plans he wouldn't have been killed. Of course, Delos was never the smartest kid he'd ever encountered. It was a wonder he survived as long as he did.

Foster, on the other hand, made the most money of the three of them. He worked on his own. Even though he took kids from foster homes, not ones under the management of Jasper's company, he also was an opportunist. He'd see a kid he liked, played with them for a while and when he got tired of using them for his own sexual pleasure, he took them to Theodore. What he did for a day job was anyone's guess. He must have been doing something to stay off the radar, at least until the ranch was raided and the survivors were remembering what happened to them as children and teenagers.

The latest news came when Foster was arrested. It made him glad he was able to move to a different foster facility, where no one was privy to his side job for Theodore.

He was just getting ready to go his rented room in town, when his communicator beeped with a message. It didn't come as a surprise to see Jasper's face on his screen.

"Did you hear about Foster?" his friend asked.

"That dumb bastard should have signed on with us. It's too bad someone didn't off him like that guy did to Delos."

"Don't get too cocky, Noah. It's a good thing you got a job at a different facility. Just lay low. Thankfully, I made a deal with Theo and he kept my name out of everything, at least that's what he told me."

"I understand. I was able to get a job with another company. It was good of you to give me such a glowing recommendation."

"Just remember, lay low and keep your mouth shut. We don't want those damn aliens breathing down our necks. I have no desire to go to one of those penal colonies like Theo and Granger."

Jasper broke the connection, leaving Noah with more questions than answers. He was certain no one would be able to find him.

"That's him," he heard the manager of the facility say. "That's Noah Hammer."

He looked up and saw two men, who could only be Aliens. For a moment he thought about hightailing it to his hovercraft, but it was too late. He'd already been pointed out to them. From what he heard; he didn't have a snowball's chance in hell of out running them.

"Noah Hammer," the taller of the two men called out.

Turning to face the men, he strode to where they were standing. "I'm Noah Hammer, what can I do for you?"

He held out his hand in greeting but his gesture was ignored.

"You are under arrest. You have the right to an attorney, if you cannot afford one, one will be appointed to you. Be aware that anything you say may be used against you in a court of law."

Before he could comprehend what, the man said or protest it, electronic cuffs were attached to his wrists.

"What charges are there against me?" he finally managed to ask.

"The charges are kidnapping and human trafficking. We are here to transport you first to the Kansas City Complex, then to the complex in Nevada for trial."

"Trial? Isn't that a bit hasty?"

"Not for the severity of the charges against you. We have evidence that you not only kidnapped young boys, but you were paid by Theodore Henderson for your activities."

"What about my hover craft?"

"Where you're going you won't need it. We will impound it until after your trial. It will be kept safe at the Kansas City Complex."

Noah made no further attempt at conversation. The only way they could have associated him with the kidnappings was if Foster spilled his guts. The Aliens caught up with him in Illinois. It was completely possible he was being held in Nevada right now. Even though they'd been friends, he wouldn't put it past Foster to rat him out in order to save his own ass. He'd make it his priority to find out what he told these freaks even if he had to beat the shit out of him.

Well, it didn't matter what they did to him, there was no way he was going to implicate Jasper. He respected the older man who arranged for him to have job opportunities ever since they devised the plan to keep Theo supplied with unwanted boys after he aged out of the program at Henderson Ranch.

~ * ~

Foster Warren cursed the Aliens who brought him here, the ones who were his jailers, and the suck ass lawyer they appointed for him. He wondered how in the hell they'd found him in the first place.

The only thing that he approved of was the way the Alien who came to arrest him collapsed. With any luck the bastard died before they could get him medical attention. From what he'd heard they came to Earth about seventy-five years ago. Well, as far as he was concerned, they could go back to where they came from.

He thought about the business he'd engaged in with Theodore. It was good money while it lasted. Of course, the side benefit was that he used the boys he kidnapped for his own pleasure for several days, weeks, or months before he turned them over to Theodore.

He remembered working with Delos for a while, but the idiot wasn't an opportunist like he was. He never had to involve anyone other than himself. It amazed him that Delos was able to find people who wanted kids to disappear and pay him to do the dirty work. Whatever, he was lucky not to get mixed up with someone like the bastard who killed Delos, to get the entire amount Theodore paid for the kids.

It came as a surprise when the guards brought in two more prisoners. Even though he hadn't seen Jasper in over thirty years, he would have known him anywhere. It was the same with Noah. It made him wonder how they were caught.

"I should have known it was you," Jasper shouted as he was taken into the cell next to Foster's. "What kind of deal did you make with them? How could you have sicked those bastards onto me?"

"I haven't told them anything. I'm still trying to figure out how they found me. Maybe you should be asking your questions of your buddy, Noah."

"I already have. It seems that we weren't arrested until after they had you in custody. How else would they have connected us with that fiasco Theo ran on the ranch?"

"You knew what was going on there, just like I did. He wasn't paying all that money for those kids if he wasn't making an even larger profit on them when they aged out, to say nothing of the money he got every month from the state of Nevada. To them he was a godsend for taking on kids no one wanted. Did you get as much pleasure from them as I did before I took them to the ranch?"

"You have a filthy mind. I've never touched a child in my life.

You were the one who liked to diddle with little boys."

Foster smiled as he thought about all the kids he'd enjoyed over the years. Theodore wasn't his only customer. He also worked for several pimps who wanted little girls to groom to become prostitutes. From what he heard, they had a growing business, selling girls who ranged in age from ten to twelve and who had been trained correctly to pleasure men all over the world. He would find girls of about three or four years old. They were easy marks, especially when they were out shopping with their mothers. It didn't take long for him to snatch a kid when the mother was busy shopping or had sent the kid out to play. He enjoyed playing with the girls as much as he did the boys. They all screamed and cried at first, but by the time he was ready to sell them off, they learned to like the things he did to them.

Thinking about the children, he remembered how Theodore's mother often asked him to come up to the house to help with the housework. He soon learned, she liked it when he fondled her and sucked on her breasts. That was what he did with the girls. It was Theodore's father who showed him the pleasure of being fondled and sucking on the older man's penis. He'd used all this training when he went out on his own to procure kids for all of his customers.

~ * ~

Noah was horrified when he learned they would be taken to Resurrection Ranch for the trial. The last thing he wanted to do was to face the kids he'd sold to Theodore. To him they were little more than mindless slaves. He knew how they were treated on the ranch. They were groomed to be able to get along on little or no food as well as to become good slaves.

Yes, Theodore had quite the little business going. He got money from the state for taking in unwanted children. By the time they turned five, they were treated like slaves and taught to do carpentry and ranching. When they aged out, he made a hefty profit selling them off. Not only that, he also made good money off the prime beef he raised and sold off. Looking back on things, he should have asked for more money for the brats he took to Nevada. It made him wonder how many assets Theodore amassed before he was caught.

Chapter Twelve

Things moved faster than anyone ever expected them to. Within twenty-four hours of the meeting held in the dining hall, word came that Noah Hammer had been apprehended and was being held at the Nevada Complex in anticipation of being transferred to a secure facility close to Resurrection Ranch.

Mark was in his office when he received the news of the capture. Ever since he came into his office this morning, he'd been receiving communications from the various facilities about Noah Hammer and the many jobs he held at various foster home facilities. He'd worked in Iowa, Minnesota, Wisconsin and Illinois. Upon checking, they found the facilities were all owned and operated by the same company. The CEO of the company, had been arrested when his affiliation with Henderson Ranch was discovered. Even if he hadn't been the one who carried out the kidnappings, communications between him and Hendersons were incriminating.

Mark could feel his stomach begin to roil. He wanted this nightmare over as soon as possible, in order to get on with educating the former residents of Henderson Ranch. After last night's meeting, he'd met with Parker and Clint regarding the future of the ranch. They both expressed an interest in bringing troubled youth to the ranch. It was surprising, since this was the dream that Chris told him about when they met for the first time at the Denver Complex. What began as a dream was set to become a reality, sooner than any of them ever anticipated.

A knock at his office door brought him back to the here and now. To his surprise, his visitors turned out to be Peter of the oldest of their group of 'Lost Boys'.

"What's wrong?" Mark asked.

"Nothing's wrong," Peter said. "After last night we've been talking and we were surprised when Parker and Clint said they wanted to look into turning this into a rehab for troubled youth. We all think this is one of the best suggestions we've heard since we were rescued.

"I've been looking into things," Peter commented, continuing the conversation. "There are a lot of kids who could use a place like this, and not just boys. Since we brought in the girls, we could have a completely coeducational facility. This is what I've wanted to do ever since I was rescued. We can do this and not just in the future. We talked to Cassion and he completely agrees with the project. Of course, he can't be doing as much as he'd like to but there are several mentors who are qualified to make it happen."

Momentarily, Mark was overwhelmed. The dream he'd been contemplating earlier, was going to come to fruition. He prayed he would be up to a project of such magnitude.

~ * ~

After her morning class, Josie waited in her classroom for her first history class with Caroline. From what little she'd gleaned from the media about the history of this country as well as the world, she was hungry for more knowledge. She always knew the stories handed down by the One God through the Bible, but there had to be so very much more.

"I'm sorry if I'm late," Caroline said, when she entered the room. "The nanny who cares for Johnathan while we work, was running behind today. We will still have plenty of time for our class."

"I didn't know your husband worked. What does he do?"

"He's a librarian by trade, so he is invaluable in getting things set up here. He's been combing the libraries for any and all books they are willing to send to us. When he ran the library in Chicago, he always had several copies of books. He often shared what he wasn't using with other libraries who were in need. The response has been overwhelming. In a few weeks, he should have the library here at the educational center filled and ready for people to check them out. Unfortunately, there were no history books, but when I arrived at the Denver complex, I took over that job."

Josie could feel her eyes widen with anticipation. She loved reading and looked forward to having access to a library. Among her things, she'd found several novels that she loved reading, but she was hungry for new books like the ones she read from the library in Maquoketa.

"Does he need any help?" she asked, anxiously.

"He appreciates any help he can get, but I'm afraid you might be spreading yourself too thin. Not only are you teaching your classes, but you are stepping in for Hodia until Astra can make arrangements to get here. That along with your class with me, you might not be able to find the time to spend with a special young man."

A blush creeped into Josie's cheeks. "My brother told me this was a small community and there were few secrets. I guess he was right. I have been seeing Clint when we have time either at dinner or on the weekend. I realize he has to study at night after our classes and so do I. Any time we have together comes at a premium. I do have time in the afternoons and working with books would be more of a relaxing adventure than work. Can you ask him if he would mind me helping him?"

"I'll ask and see what he says. Now, let's get to work on your history lesson."

Josie sat at one of the desks where her early morning class sat earlier. From her bag, she retrieved her laptop in order to take notes.

"There are centuries of history that have been lost or eradicated over the years. Since I know next to nothing about the history from 2020 to 2120, I will start with the history I remember from 2020 and go backward. I'd appreciate it if you closed your laptop. I want you to listen to what I have to say. I have a copy of the important points that I will be emailing to your computer after class. For now, it's best if you aren't distracted by the electronics."

Closing her laptop came as a surprise to Josie. All through her elementary, secondary and college education, she'd used it to take notes. As she thought about it, she typed as she listened not realizing that until she reviewed her notes, she had no idea what her teachers and professors actually said.

"Good. It was in 2020 that the Covid 19 Virus reared its ugly head in China. My husband was there on a business trip and was one of the first victims of the disease. I was so afraid of contracting it, I decided to go into suspended animation or cryogenics as it was called then. Prior to that the world was in turmoil. The United States consisted of fifty states, but the disasters I'm told that hit the east and west coasts changed all that.

"In this country, President Trump was in the White House and was planning to run for a second term. There were riots brought about by people who were pro Trump and wanted to make him either a dictator or a king. Democracy was in jeopardy. There were several race riots of white against black and visa-versa. At the same time, we were fighting in Afghanistan and the Middle East, but I'll touch more on that later."

Josie was amazed at how much she absorbed by just listening, then by trying to take notes. All too soon, the lesson ended. She suddenly realized that they'd only covered the first twenty years of the twenty-first century. Hearing about the events of 9/11 with the bombings of the Twin Towers in New York, the Pentagon in Washington, D.C. and the crashing of another plane in a field in Pennsylvania, brought tears to her eyes.

"How could people be so cruel to each other?"

Caroline grew somber. "Like I said, it was a time when the world was in turmoil. It's also the reason the Aliens made their presence known. Unfortunately, by the time they arrived, the damage to history had been done. I think it's the reason I was found. My background was in history and I knew the history of this country very well. As for the ancient history, it was what I studied in college. Without the knowledge I had, the world still wouldn't know what happened in the past and learned from it. Unfortunately, our time for today is up. Check out the material I sent to your email. It should cover things in much further detail. Tomorrow, we will delve into the last twenty years of the twentieth century. I have a feeling I have overwhelmed you with enough information for one day."

Josie agreed. Just the minute amount of history she'd heard about today boggled her mind. From what she heard; the world went through many changes throughout history. She'd even been told the slavery that her brother as well as the young men who were rebuilding Resurrection Ranch were forced into was not something new to the world. It existed since the beginning of time. It was just that people did their best to forget the past.

~ * ~

Word about the proposed expansion of the ranch to bring in kids who weren't brought up here spread like wildfire. Clint was surprised when one of the Native American cowboys mentioned it as they rode in for dinner that night.

"Parker and I talked about doing this and were surprised when we learned it was the original dream of Chris' and everything seemed to grow."

"Where we come from, we would have called it snowballing," one of their companions commented.

"Snowballing? What's that?" Clint asked.

"That's right, you've probably never seen snow, at least not that you would remember. In Montana, where we come from, snow starts falling in late October or early November and continues through April or May. It's basically frozen moisture. I'm told, in the old days when it would snow, our people used it as a time for rest. Of course, during the twenty and twenty-first centuries, no one remembered the old ways of our people. If it weren't for the story tellers, we would have never known what the lives of our ancestors were like."

Clint could see visions of what once was. The people who were the owners of this ranch were a noble race. He'd heard many stories from these men who rode with them. In a way he wished he'd been born hundreds of years in the past to live like the men who had quickly become good friends. He wondered if he would have been a warrior or a hunter. Would he have provided food for his tribe or been a leader? He doubted the leader part. It was possible, he would have been one of many who worked for the good of the entire tribe. He could envision Chris as an ancient warrior or even a chief.

"You look like you're deep in thought," Parker said, as he urged his horse to slow down in order for Clint to catch up.

"I guess I am. I was wondering what this country was like before the white men came and destroyed so many different tribes. I've been riding with Joseph White Horse and he's been telling me about the stories of his people."

"I know," Parker agreed. "I've been listening to Samuel Red Dog and he's been telling me the same stories. I wonder what it would have been like before…well, you know."

"That's something we will never know. To hear our Native American friends, talk, it was an ideal time. They were princes of the plains. They rode horses and lived off the land. From the stories I've heard, they also had slaves, like we were. Joseph said that the tribes waged wars against each other and took prisoners who were sold as slaves. Guess it wasn't just us who have been exploited. I'm anxious to learn history when we start our secondary education."

Chapter Thirteen

The trial for Foster, Noah and Jasper, was set for a week after they arrived in Nevada. The ranch was geared up for the event. While all the 'Lost Boys' were in attendance, the Native Americans worked as a skeleton crew.

To everyone's surprise several of the boys and men who had been reunited with their families, were also in attendance. The most dramatic entry was Foster Warren's fraternal twin brother being wheeled into the gymnasium that had been transformed into a courtroom. The defendants were being held in the locker room where they could be secured.

The seats that had been brought in were all filled. As the defendants came into the room, a hush fell over everyone assembled to witness the proceedings and to give testimony against the three men.

Because of Cassion's condition, a prosecutor from the Nevada facility was the first to make his opening statement.

"As you can see, we have assembled a jury of twelve individuals, with no connection to either Henderson Ranch or as it is called today, Resurrection Ranch. These three men were involved in a profitable industry of kidnapping and trafficking young boys. Over the past thirty years, many children have been brought here by Foster Warren and Noah Hammer. The third defendant, Jasper Constantine was the CEO of a large network of foster homes, where many of the children were procured. There is a fourth defendant who should be here, but unfortunately, he was killed over twenty years ago.

"While Noah Hammer took boys from the foster homes, run by the board of directors' led by Jasper Constantine, Foster Warren chose children randomly. Not only did he kidnap boys. He also took little girls to be trained to be prostitutes or sold into the sex trade as small children. As for Delos Reynolds, the man who was killed, he worked for benefactors who were interested in making children disappear.

"Through files found at the ranch, we have discovered the Henderson's kept meticulous records. We have learned which boy was taken by which of these defendants and how much they were paid. With further digging it was discovered the organization run by Jasper Constantine, was paid over fifty thousand dollars a year."

The lawyer for Noah Hammer was the first to make an opening statement. "My client is little more than a physical laborer. He worked for Jasper Constantine as a groundskeeper and did only what Mr. Constantine ordered him to do. He was brought up on this ranch and in his estimation, he had a wonderful childhood. It is our contention that he was giving these children a better life."

The lawyers for each of the other two defendants both gave the same opening statement. It was as though they were actors who memorized exactly what they were going to say.

The first prosecution witness was Frederick Warren. After swearing to tell the truth, he wheeled his chair, so he was sitting in front of the witness box.

"Can you state your name and your connection to these defendants?" Darien, the prosecuting attorney asked.

"My name is Frederick Warren. Foster Warren is my fraternal twin brother. When our parents were killed, we were sent to Henderson Ranch. At that time, it was run by Robert Henderson, the father of Theodore Henderson. When Robert, or Bob as he wanted us to call him, ran the ranch, it was a decent place to grow up. We had good food and a great primary education. When it was time for us to move on to high school, he drove us into town every morning and picked us up every afternoon. After graduation, we were each offered a college education at his expense. I was the only one who took him up on his offer."

"Other than yourself and your brother, who else was at the ranch?"

"There were several young men. What paths they took in their lives I never knew. My close friends were Theodore Henderson, Paul Grainger, Delos Reynolds, Noah Hammer, Jasper Constantine and of course, my brother Foster.

"After I graduated from college, I had little to no contact with any of them, with the exception of my brother. He would pop up every few years when he needed money. Other than that, I didn't know about anything that went on at Henderson Ranch, until the raid was made on the facility and the trials for Theodore Henderson and Paul Grainger were held. I was appalled by the atrocities my former friends perpetuated here. I know if Robert and Mary Henderson were still alive none of these things would have happened. The young men and boys who were brought here would have been actual orphans or children who had been abandoned."

At the table for the defendants, the three attorneys conferred before the man who was defending Foster, got to his feet for the cross examination.

"Mr. Warren, why is it that you are testifying against your brother?"

"Because it's the proper thing to do. Until the trials for Theodore and Paul were held, I had no idea what was going on here. Just recently, I was visited by a man with the name of Cassion. I immediately recognized him, from seeing him at the trials I watched on my communicator. He came to my home, thinking I was Foster and I'd changed my name. When I confirmed that I was Foster's twin brother, he asked me where my brother could be found. I told him, the last I knew he was somewhere in Illinois. If that's how he located Foster, I was glad to help."

"You said you were brought up on this ranch, like the others. Are we to believe you weren't involved in the crimes our clients are accused of?"

"I took advantage of the education Bob Henderson offered me. I got a fantastic education that led to a good job opportunity. Had it not been for an unfortunate accident at my workplace, I would still be working there. As you can see, I am confined to this chair."

"You bastard," Foster said getting to his feet. "You sold me out. I knew it had to be you."

The judge banged his gavel and several of the police officers, who were in the courtroom, forced him back into his seat and restrained him there.

When Frederick was excused, a second witness was called to the stand. To everyone's surprise, it was Zander Rawlins.

After stating his full name, he began his testimony. "I am not one of the kids who lived through hell while growing up here. I know nothing of any of the three defendants. It was Delos Reynolds who changed my life and the lives of my family forever, when I was five and my younger brother, Jake, disappeared from a family outing. We were contacted, right after the raid on Henderson Ranch. At the time we were told Jake had been brought here and died when he was still a teenager. My father had always been angry about Jake's disappearance. When we learned what happened, he insisted I wage war on the ranch. I'm ashamed to say that I rustled cattle from this ranch and set fire to one of the outbuildings. The fact that I'd been badly burned in the fire, brought my parents and sister to this ranch.

"While I was still hospitalized, my father finally had a psychotic break and killed one of the young men who knew my brother. At the same time, he wounded several others. Instead of blaming Delos Reynolds for what happened, he turned his anger on the ranch."

Another of the defense attorneys got to her feet.

"You say you and your father committed terrible crimes against this ranch. If that is the case, why are you free to testify at this trial?"

"I'm not free. Once I realized how wrong everything my father told me over the years was, I threw myself on the mercy of the young men and women who are building up this ranch. I have agreed not to leave the ranch for the next five years. I am working with the people here, to make this a caring place for troubled boys and girls. As for my father, he has been committed to an asylum for the criminally insane. It breaks my heart that his mind was so filled with hatred he murdered one of my brother's best friends.

"Although my brother died before he had a chance to live, I've been told he was one of the lucky ones. He didn't have to suffer the horrors of being sold to one of the slave ranches in Mexico or one of the skinhead groups. Hearing the stories these young men have told me, I completely agree with them.

"Coming here has completely changed my life. I look forward to helping these young men to rebuild this to a ranch that they can take pride in."

Once Zander finished his testimony, the proceeding adjourned for the noon meal.

~ * ~

Patsy, Diane, Connor and Julie worked preparing lunch for everyone attending the trial. As they worked, they watched the proceedings on the large monitor that had been installed in the kitchen.

"I don't mind cooking for the extra people who are here, but why do we have to cater to the three men who brought so much grief to so many of the young men on this ranch," Patsy commented. "If it were up to me, I'd take them some of the slop the Hendersons fed those kids."

Conner laughed at her comment. "You know we can't do that. If we did, it wouldn't make us any better than the monsters who ran this ranch as a slave operation for so many years. Granted, they won't be getting steak and lobster, but I did make them some nourishing soup and bread."

Patsy shook her head. She didn't agree with feeding them anything nourishing, but she knew treating them in the same way the Hendersons treated the boys who were brought here was wrong.

~ * ~

Connor could understand what Patsy was saying, but at the same time, he knew he couldn't withhold food from the defendants.

After loading trays with soup and bread, as well as steaming cups of coffee, he, along with Julie and Diane, headed over to the gym to deliver the food to the locker room where the prisoners were being held.

At the door, they were met by Jason Culver. "If it were up to me, I'd give these jerks bread and water."

"I know," Connor replied. "I just had this same conversation with Patsy. It's not bread and water, but just a step up. I made them some soup and fresh baked bread along with coffee. I promise I didn't put poison in it."

Jason smiled. "You're right of course. Were you able to watch this morning's session?"

Connor nodded. "Listening to what Frederick and Zander had to say, convinced me of their guilt. Of course, there are more people who will be testifying this afternoon, to say nothing of the next few days."

Jason unlocked the door and went in with Connor and Diane.

"What's this crap?" Jasper asked.

"It's better than you deserve," Diane replied. "Compared with what the boys you brought here were fed, this is a feast fit for a king."

"Feast?" Foster echoed. "I bet this slop isn't what's being served to everyone else who is here."

"It's not, but it's better than you deserve," Connor said. "I should have let some of the boys you brought here serve you, but I'm afraid they would kill you for what you did to them. Do the names Brad King and Clint Anders mean anything to you?"

Connor could see the color drain from Noah's face. He'd struck a nerve. Turning his attention to Jasper, he could see the recognition of the names in his eyes.

"Maybe I should have sent in Parker Flint, Norman Priestly and Dan Campion."

Ever since the names of the men who sold boys to the ranch had been revealed, Parker and Dan recalled being taken by Foster, from their parents. It had been Parker and Dan who recalled Foster being their abductor. As for anything else they remembered from that time, they were reluctant to say more.

An icy silence settled on the room, as the trays were placed on the table in front of each of the prisoners.

"I need to get to back to the dining hall, to serve the noon meal."

As Connor and Diane left the room, he prayed he would have triggered some remorse within the three men.

~ * ~

"You look a little sick, Foster," Jasper commented. "Couldn't be that you're worried about what those brats might say, are you?"

Foster looked up. "I'm not worried about what they might say.

103

Parker and Dan were too young to remember anything that was done to them before I brought them here. As I recall, they were sweet little morsels. Of all the kids I took, they were the best. Especially Dan. He was a chubby little fellow and what I taught that boy to do with his mouth almost prompted me to keep him. Unfortunately, the money Theodore had waiting for me was more important. It was so much I couldn't turn it down."

"You are one sick bastard," Noah accused. "I took those boys, but I never used them. That is just morally wrong."

"Don't give me that shit, Noah. We all knew that selling those kids to Theo was going to ruin their lives, that is if they lived long enough to have lives. I watched Theo's trial and I heard about the kids they found buried on the property. Even with all the crappy things the Hendersons did to me, they didn't kill any of us. We were fed well and given an education. I don't know where Theo got his warped ideas for this place, but I can tell you he made a boatload of money. We all profited from what he was doing here too. If you were such a wuss that you didn't take advantage of those sweet little bodies, that's your problem, not mine."

Rather than continue their conversation, Foster tasted his soup. He had to admit it wasn't half bad. Also on the plate were two slices of freshly made bread slathered with butter. Even the coffee tasted better than anything he made when he was doing his own cooking.

~ * ~

The afternoon session was called to order. The first witness to take the stand was Clint. After stating his name and age, he began to tell his story.

"Until I heard the name of Noah Hammer, I had little memory of what occurred before I was brought here. Hearing his name seemed to bring back the forgotten memories, including my time at the foster home.

"I was pretty little when my mom abandoned me. The story they told me at the foster home, was that she'd been arrested and sent to prison, leaving me with a neighbor. When she could no longer care for me, she called the authorities to have me taken to the foster home.

"I didn't like it there, but I was too little to make my feelings known. There was a man there, he said his name was Noah Hammer and he was the gardener. One day, he said he was going to take me on a trip. I thought he was treating me to something special. Instead, he brought me to Henderson Ranch. Mr. Henderson said that I belonged to him, bought and paid for. I didn't know what that meant, but I learned soon enough."

"Can you explain what you meant?"

Clint took a deep breath and made eye contact with Josie. "I was young enough that I didn't have to work right away, but I soon learned I would never get enough to eat. When I turned five, I started riding the range with the men. From what I've been told, I should have been going to school, but that wasn't part of the plan. I learned how to write my name and do simple arithmetic as well as how to become a rancher. From the time Noah brought me here until I turned eighteen, I was never allowed to leave this ranch.

"I was about fifteen when one of my best friends, Jake Rawlins, went off to chase a steer that had broken away from the herd. When he returned, Henderson was with us and he put Jake in the box for fifteen hours, one hour for each year of his life. By the time Henderson let him out of the box, he was dead. As far as I'm concerned, he was the lucky one.

"When I turned eighteen, I was sold to a slave ranch in Mexico that made this place look like paradise. Three of us turned eighteen at the same time. Parker Flint, Roger Blount and I were all sold to the same ranch. How we survived in order to be rescued, I don't know."

"Where are Parker and Roger now?"

Clint didn't know if he had the strength to answer the prosecutor's question. Gall threatened to choke off any words he might have wanted to speak. It was hard enough talking about Jake's death, but to tell about how Roger's life ended seemed to be asking too much of him.

"Please answer the question, Mr. Anders," the judge said.

Clint forced the gall back down his throat.

"We were all rescued, but since they couldn't find our parents, we were taken to the Alien Complex in Mexico City. It was there we were approached by Peter. We knew he was on the same ranch as we were, but we were on different crews. We never saw much of him.

"We all agreed to return to help rebuild Resurrection Ranch. Parker and I have been talking about opening this ranch to troubled kids, both male and female and teaching them a good work ethic while they get their educations."

"What about Roger?"

"Roger is dead. Jake's father had such a hatred for what happened to his son here. When he cracked, he came into the dining hall and killed Roger."

"What do you know about Jasper Constantine?"

"Nothing until I heard Brad tell the same story of how Noah Hammer took him from the foster home. That was when I put two and two together. I figured out that someone from the foster home was behind the abductions. From the books that Henderson kept, I found I was taken from a foster home in Wisconsin and Brad was taken from Minnesota. We dug deeper into the records that we found in the office and realized payments were being made to Jasper Constantine. It didn't take long to find out he was the CEO of the chain of foster homes where we were both taken from to be brought here."

The attorney for Noah Hammer got to his feet. "How is it that you accuse my client of wrongdoing?"

"He kidnapped me from the foster home and sold me to Henderson. At the time I didn't know that he got money, but the longer I was here, the more kids I saw being sold to Henderson, by Hammer, Warren and Reynolds. I might not have had an education, but I wasn't stupid. I saw the money that changed hands."

It seemed as though his answer took the wind out of the defense attorney's sails. As he took his seat the attorney for Jasper took over.

"You say you don't know my client, but yet you are implicating him in this case. How can that be?"

"I'm not implicating him. It was the records kept by the Hendersons kept that implicated him. They kept complete records about what they paid for each boy, how much he received from the state of Nevada and how much he sold them for when they turned eighteen. It showed that your client was paid fifteen hundred after each boy was purchased and three thousand when they were resold. If I hadn't realized Brad and I were taken by the same person from a foster home, it would have never prompted the Mentors from the Alien community to search further into the records."

With no further questions forthcoming, Clint was excused. He immediately took the seat next to Josie.

"You were fantastic," she whispered, squeezing his hand reassuringly.

"I told the truth as I knew it. It was hard when I could see Noah staring at me. Visions of the man taking me from the security of the foster home to the hell of Henderson Ranch played-out in my mind's eye. I had to force the vision from my mind in order to be able to complete my testimony."

~ * ~

Parker was the next one to take the stand. As soon as he was seated in the witness chair, he made eye contact with Foster Warren. Seeing the monster of his dreams in person, brought to the forefront memories of what Foster did to him when he first took him away from his mother and father. After stating his name and age, he began to tell his story.

"My story began when I was shopping with my parents. I was just a little kid, but they were looking at something that didn't interest me. I wanted to see the toys. Foster was there and he bought me a truck I wanted. He told me he was going to get me a hot dog, so I went with him. I never got the hot dog. Instead, he put me in his hover craft and took me away from the store.

"When he finally docked, it was in front of a run-down shack. I asked him when I was going to get my hot dog, because my folks would be worried about me. He told me I'd get a wiener when we got into the house. Instead of getting me something to eat, he exposed himself to me. He pointed at his penis and said I was to suck it. When I said no, he forced me to do it again and again. When he came in my mouth, he told me to swallow it. I puked it back up, and that made him laugh. That was when he took my clothes off and stuck his finger up my butt. It hurt, but when

I cried, he pushed even harder. He told me that's what men and boys did when they were together.

"He kept me at the shack for what seemed like forever before he put me in his hover craft, and we ended up at Henderson Ranch. I saw Mr. Henderson give him a lot of cash, at least in my mind it was a lot of money. That was when the real hell began. We were fed slop and as soon as I turned five, I started riding with the older boys watching over the cattle.

"When I turned eighteen, Mr. Henderson sent me into town with one hundred dollars. That was when I met Paul Granger and his wife. The morning after I got there, Mr. Granger, took me to Mexico. Before nightfall, I'd been fitted with a shock collar, branded and put in isolation for two weeks. I worked there with my friends, Roger and Clint, until we were rescued when the aliens raided the ranch."

When he paused, the prosecuting attorney got to his feet. "Can you explain what you mean when you say you were branded?"

Without thinking, Parker pushed up the shirt sleeve on his left arm, to show the brand for the Flying A ranch, owned by Sr. Alfonso. "I was his property, just like the cattle and horses."

To his surprise, Peter and Clint also got to their feet and pushed up their left shirt sleeves to show everyone in the room, their brands that were identical to the one Parker just displayed. Throughout the courtroom, there was an audible gasp from the spectators and the jurors at the horror the three of them displayed. Even the three defendants and their lawyers looked shocked to see them branded as ranchers did for their livestock.

From the jury box, as well as the spectators, he could hear women and men choking back sobs. What was as natural as breathing to him seemed to be horrifying to the people in the room.

The judge banged his gavel and ordered everyone to take their seats.

Once Parker was seated, the lawyer for Foster Warren got to his feet. "How can you be so certain that my client is the man who took you from the store where your parents were shopping? You admit you were but a small child."

"He told me his name and I read it again when I was going through the records the Henderson's left."

"You read it? From what you and the other witnesses have told us, you were deprived of an education. If that is true, how is it you can read anything? Aren't you nothing more than an ignorant cow puncher? Isn't it true that you have the mentality of a three-year-old?"

Parker could feel his blood began to boil. He knew he had to remain calm. "When I left this ranch at the age of eighteen, I wasn't book smart, but I knew more than a three-year-old could ever comprehend. Since my rescue, I have been given the education I deserved as a child. I may not have the college education that you have, but I'm learning more and more every day. At the Mexico City Complex, I was able to begin my formal education. Here on the ranch, I take classes in the evening from Miss Josie. I should be able to test out of the elementary program at the end of the semester and start my secondary education. I'm proud of what I've accomplished. My only regret is that I was never able to reconnect with my parents. It's as though they've disappeared off the face of the earth."

By the time he finished his testimony, it was time for court to adjourn for the evening. Getting down from the stand, Parker was completely drained. Even though he felt as though someone turned on a faucet and drained out his energy, he held his head high and didn't let on to how exhausted he felt as he left the makeshift courtroom.

With the afternoon session finished, the prisoners were taken back to the locker room and secured for the night. They were told supper would be served to them, but not to think about trying to escape, as the only exit from the room was locked and heavily guarded.

"What kind of a fool are you?" Jasper asked, once he heard the lock click. "Why in the hell did you tell that brat your real name? Didn't you know it was going to come back and bite you in the ass?"

"You can call me what you want," Foster replied. "I knew what was going on at this ranch and I figured the brat wouldn't live long enough to ever leave here. If he did, he'd be sold to someone who would either starve him or work him to death. Who knew the Aliens would get involved and find out what Henderson was doing with the kids we brought here? If they'd kept their nose out of things, we could have continued to fly under the radar and never get caught."

"I've been thinking about Delos. I wonder what he was getting for selling kids their families didn't want. I talked to him once, well over twenty-five years ago, and he told me although he did some snatch and run with kids, it was nothing like you were, Foster. He also told me that he found it to be much more lucrative to find people who had kids they wanted to have disappear. If he was such a dim bulb, how did he ever come up with such a scheme."

"That doesn't matter now," Jasper said. "He wasn't smart enough to know the last guy he trusted was going to murder him. He was a dumb shit, but he got onto something he thought was going to be good. Unfortunately, it cost him his life when he hooked up with the wrong guy."

Hearing the electronic lock on the door click, silenced the conversation between the three prisoners.

Jasper was pleased to see the man who came earlier with their midday meal. Although he expected more of the soup from earlier, he was surprised to see they were being served a full meal with meat, potatoes, vegetables and coffee.

Chapter Fourteen

Sharday, the mentor for Betsy Potts, was shocked when she picked Betsy up from school. The little girl, who usually was full of the exciting things she'd learned that day, was crying bitterly.

"What's wrong?" Sharday asked.

"I'm scared."

"What are you scared about, sweetheart?"

"I heard about the trial for the men who took the boys and brought them here. I'm afraid the man named Foster will come and find me."

"How do you know about him?"

"He's the one who sold me to Master. He did terrible things to me and told Master he could continue to do the same things to me. He hurt me and when I cried, he did it again and again. I don't want him to find me and do it to me anymore."

Sharday was taken aback. "Do you know if he brought the other girls to Master?"

Betsy sobbed even louder and nodded her head. "He brought some of us there. They told me what he did to them and I understood why they didn't like doing what Master asked them to do. A lot of them were older than us."

Tears welled in Sharday's eyes, but she forced them back. After reassuring Betsy that she was safe now, she sent a message on her communicator to Nova and Zakaria the mentors for Lydia Morgan and Rachael Steed. They all needed to talk and see if they remembered the same experiences as Betsy did.

After several minutes of text messages between her counterparts and the mentors for the young boys. Sharada agreed the six of them should meet, but not until their wards were in their respective classes for the day. She knew it was going to be a hard night and she wouldn't be getting much sleep. In preparation for the long night ahead of her, she found a book she'd received from her parents before she made the long journey from under the Antarctician ice cap to the Alien complex outside of Indianapolis, Indiana.

Together with Betsy, she went to the dining hall, hopeful that she had successfully put a smile on her face. It would do no good for anyone to know of her suspicions about the three men who were on trial before she had a chance to talk to her counterparts about what their charges might have said.

~ * ~

The mood in the dining hall was subdued when Parker entered. The trial, with the explicit details he'd revealed for the first time in his life, had been sobering. He prayed none of his friends would think less of him for what he'd testified to earlier in the day. Even though it was necessary in order to convict the man who abused him before selling him to Henderson, he felt dirty.

Clint and Josie were sitting at a table on the far side of the room. He saw Clint motion him over and he returned his friend's gesture with a nod of his head.

He was standing in line to get his meal, when he saw Sharday enter with her charge. He remembered the day they first arrived at the ranch. The child had a vacant look in her eyes. It was a look he knew all too well. If he could have seen himself when he first came to the ranch, he knew he would have seen the same look mirrored in his eyes.

Tonight, it seemed as though the little girl had been crying and her mentor, Sharday, appeared to be overly protective of her charge.

The mentors for the three little girls intrigued him. They carried themselves well and their exotic appearance was entrancing. He'd always wanted to approach Sharday, but knew he could never be good enough for someone like her.

In truth, he was no more than the ignorant cowpuncher the defense lawyer accused him of being earlier in the day.

With his plate filled, he made his way to the table where Clint and Josie waited for him.

"You did well in court today," Clint said. "I can't believe the abuse you endured before you came here."

"Up until now, it was more of a nightmare than anything else. I didn't actually remember any of it until I saw his name on the paperwork we found in the office. It all came back to me and I knew the nightmares actually happened to me."

Josie covered his hand with hers. "I wish none of this would have ever happened to any of you, but we are all here to make a difference. You got the process started with your testimony today."

"I know I did. There is something that is bothering me. Do you think it's possible that one or more of these guys was kidnapping little girls for the sex trafficking trade?"

He watched as Clint pondered the question he'd just posed.

"I hadn't thought about that, but it's entirely possible. Thinking back to when the girls were brought here, I remember the vacant look in their eyes. They were abused, whether by one of these creeps or the man they called Master, it doesn't make any difference. Hopefully, we can turn their lives around and help them to put the past behind them."

Before Parker could answer, he received a message on his communicator.

This is Sharday. Is it possible for you to meet with me and the other mentors of the young children tomorrow morning at eight in the library?

Reading it made him turn and look toward the table where Sharday and her contemporaries were seated. As usual they sat apart from the children, but close enough to monitor their actions as well as their conversations.

"I just got the strangest message," he commented.

"I got one, too," Clint replied. "Do you think the others got one as well?"

"It's possible. Something is going on. Since court isn't scheduled until ten tomorrow morning, this might concern the proceedings."

Within minutes, Parker received messages from Chris, Mark and Peter. They were all acknowledging what he was thinking.

With the evening meal finished, Parker and Clint met with the other survivors at Mark's office.

"What do you think is going on?" Parker asked, once they were assembled.

"I think we've only scraped the tip of a very big iceberg," Mark said. "I have a feeling these guys weren't just kidnapping boys. It's entirely possible one of the three girls was abducted by one of these guys. Tomorrow's meeting should be quite interesting."

"Did you reply?" Clint asked.

"I did. I thought the two of you were possibly invited like the rest of us. I said we'd all be there along with our mentors," Chris said. "I questioned Cassion being able to attend, but he assured me that he, Hodia and Jerilyn would be able to be there was well. I totally agree, the crimes these men perpetuated goes far beyond this ranch."

~ * ~

Clint and Parker thanked the Native American cowboys for covering for them yet another day.

By the time they arrived at the library, all of the adult survivors of Henderson Ranch had assembled and were waiting for Sharday to arrive with her friends. Radon, Cassion, Hodia and Jerilyn were there as well.

When the door opened, the six mentors of the younger kids entered. From the expressions on their faces, Clint knew this was going to be an emotion packed meeting.

"I'm sure you're wondering why I asked for this meeting," Sharday began. "Last night Betsy told me that she was taken from her family by Foster Warren. She was crying and said that she was worried he'd escape and come to get her. For a little girl, what she described was pretty graphic.

"I contacted the other mentors. This morning they said each of the girls told a different story. Lydia told Nova that her mother worked for Master and he killed her because she didn't make enough money for him. Rachael told Zakaria she remembered a bad man taking her and doing bad things before he took her to Master, but she didn't know his name.

"What I'm wondering is how many other little girls were taken by these monsters? I think we need to contact the facility where Master, otherwise known as Jackson Placer, is being held and get him to tell us all he knows about this operation."

Clint felt as though he'd been punched in the gut. The thought of Foster Warren doing to little girls what he'd done to him made him sick to his stomach.

"Are you certain?" he asked.

"Positive. Betsy is absolutely terrified. I told her we would all protect her, but I don't think it helped her much."

"Do you think Placer will cooperate?" Cassion asked.

"I don't know. He wasn't very forthcoming at his trial. Even without him testifying, he was sent to the penal colony on the dark side of the moon."

"Have you been able to locate Betsy's parents?" Hodia inquired.

"We tried to locate the parents of all of the girls," Nova replied. "We were able to confirm that Lydia was, indeed, the daughter of one of his prostitutes. He freely admitted to killing her when he was in a rage. As for the Rachael and Betsy, we learned that their parents are deceased. Betsy's parents were killed in a house fire. Rachael's father died just prior to her birth and her mother was killed in a fly by shooting."

"I knew it," Parker exclaimed. "While I was in Mexico, I was told my parents were killed in a house fire. That bastard killed them. I know he did. They're all monsters, but Foster Warren is the worst."

"You don't know that for sure," Mark said.

"Don't I? I was taken by Warren, so were Betsy and Dan. Do you think it's a coincidence that our parents are all dead? I can't talk for Dan, since I don't know much of his story, but Betsy and I have that in common."

"I think you might be onto something," Brad's mentor said. "I've been trying to track down Dan's parents. What I found was that they were murdered shortly after Dan's disappearance. The three of you all remember the same guy taking you and coincidently all of your parents are dead."

"What do you suggest we do?" Radon asked.

"It hasn't been used in more than a hundred and fifty years,"

Cassion began, "but there is a truth drug that can be given. Once it's been administered, the prisoner cannot avoid telling the truth. We'd have to get permission from the high counsel. They're headquartered close to Washington, DC. I can place a call to them and we should have an answer by the end of the day."

Everyone agreed with Cassion's suggestion. Even though Parker was still angry about what he'd learned, he planned to not let it show and returned to the morning session of the trial.

~ * ~

Darian was surprised when he was stopped by Cassion on his way to the gymnasium for the morning session of the trial.

"Is there something I can help you with, Cassion?" he asked.

"Yes and no. Something has come up. Can you get the judge to postpone today's session until tomorrow?"

"I don't understand. Why would you ask that?"

"I just had a meeting with the survivors of Henderson Ranch and the mentors who have been assigned to them. We have ascertained that at least three and possibly four of them were taken by Foster Warren. That being said, the parents of each of them died, shortly after their disappearance. It has to be more than mere coincidence. I have contacted the high counsel at the Washington DC complex for permission to use the truth drug. I plan to administer it to Foster Warren. Once we have his confession, we will be charging him with at least seven counts of first-degree murder."

"That's a good reason. I'll meet with the defense attorneys as well as the judge and see what I can do. Thanks for the heads up on your assumptions.

~ * ~

Word of the postponement of the trial traveled fast on the ranch. To Frederick Warren, it came as a bit of a surprise. It was even more of a surprise when Cassion came to the apartment where he and his wife were staying.

"This is a surprise," Frederick said. "Shouldn't you be resting?"

"Perhaps I should, but I deemed it necessary to come to you in person to explain why your brother's trial was postponed. We have new information and we're certain he might have committed at least seven murders in addition to the kidnapping of four of the young people here on the ranch."

"Four? I thought there were only two."

"We learned this morning that one of the little girls remembered him taking her and abusing her before she was taken to Master. She even recognized his name. We think one of the other girls were taken by him. Both of them, as well as Dan and Parker no longer have parents to return to. They all died shortly after their children disappeared."

Fredrick rubbed his forehead. "I wish I could say you're on a wild goose chase, but since Foster and I are twins, I've always been aware of the charges against him. Even though I didn't know where he was, I knew he was living a dark life. I wouldn't, for one minute, doubt him capable of not only the crimes he's been charged with but murder as well. I am sorry to have to claim him as my brother, especially my twin."

Once Cassion left the apartment, Frederick insisted his wife take him over to the gymnasium so he could speak with his brother.

~ * ~

"You have a visitor, Warren," the officer who was guarding the door to the locker room announced.

Foster looked up. "Who the hell would be visiting me? Oh wait. I bet it's my goody two-shoes brother. What if I don't want to see him?"

"The way I see it, you don't have any other choice. If it was me, I'd be happy to get out of this room and have a visit with someone other than your friends here."

Foster knew when he needed to keep his mouth shut. He held out his hands to have the electronic cuffs attached to his wrists.

"When you put it that way, why not?"

He was led across the gymnasium to what could only be the girls' locker room. Once the door was open, he saw Frederick sitting at a table. His brother motioned for him to take a seat on the opposite side of the table.

"To what do I owe such an overdue visit from my big brother?" he asked.

"I want you to confess to your crimes and plead guilty. They're planning to charge you with seven counts of first-degree murder."

"It will be a cold day in hell before I confess to something like that. They have no evidence, no proof."

"If they have to, they will make you confess. It's best if you do it on your own."

"Go to hell. Guard, Guard, I want the hell out of here."

~ * ~

Fredrick choked back tears as the guard ushered his brother out of the room where they'd been meeting. Foster's outburst did nothing more than convince him the dark half of himself was guilty of the charges being filed against him.

It broke his heart and yet he was glad he testified against his brother earlier in the trial. He was grateful his parents hadn't lived to see what had become of his twin brother. The man was a monster. The boogie man who scared little children.

Alone in the room, he allowed the tears that threatened to fall when his brother left the room, run down his cheeks. For years he'd tried to tell himself Foster was doing his own thing and it was nothing to him. Now the truth about his brother shamed him more than anything else had in his entire life.

Chapter Fifteen

With the trial postponed until the additional charges could be filed against Foster Warren, Parker and Clint rode out with the other hands. For Clint it was good to be doing something normal.

Unfortunately, he knew it wasn't the same for Parker. Even though they shared many of the same memories of being brought up on Henderson Ranch and later sold to Senor Alfanso, there were deeply buried within his memory of the abuse he endured at the hands of Foster Warren.

"Is there anything you want to talk about, Parker?" Clint finally inquired.

"I don't know. It hurt when I found out my biological parents were dead, but nothing could compare to the buried memories I have about what Foster Warren did to me when he first took me. Now to find out he might have murdered my parents; it all seems to be too much."

"Do you think you should talk to Jerilyn about this?"

"I've been thinking about it. After our meeting this morning, Sharday mentioned the same thing."

"Sharday? That's interesting. If I remember correctly, Sharday contacted you first about the little girls. Is there something going on that I should know about?"

"There is and there isn't. I've been interested in Sharday ever since she first came to the ranch with the little girls. You know as well as I do, that I am nothing more than an ignorant cowpoke. She's highly educated and…"

"…and nothing. You're getting your education. To be truthful, you're no different from Chris and he's married to Melian. Love doesn't work that way. I should know. Josie and I are getting closer every day. I should hate her. I now realize it was her father and not Josie who killed Roger. Jake was one of our best friends, but he was also her brother. I talked to Pastor Joel about this, and he said I shouldn't hold the sins of her father against her. From what I see when you and Sharday are together, I can tell she's attracted to you as well."

"If you're right, I have a lot of thinking to do. I've always thought best when I'm working. Let's get out to where the others are and see if there's anything we can do to help them."

~ * ~

Sharday watched as Parker and Clint rode out of the complex, heading toward the outlying pastures where the cattle were being kept. She'd never felt the emotions that were now raging within her mind and body. Every time she saw him, even from a distance, she was enamored with him.

"Is something on your mind?' Nova asked.

"You know there is. Do you think I should approach Parker and tell him I have feelings for him?"

"You are a silly goose," Nova replied. "Of course, you should. I wish I could find a man who makes me smile the way you do whenever you see Parker. Have you ever thought he might think he's not good enough to profess his feelings for you?"

"I guess I haven't."

"What are you waiting for? When he comes back in for supper, you need to find time to be alone with him. I will look after Betsy for you.

Sharday appreciated Nova. They'd both come from under the ice cap of Antarctica and had been lifelong friends.

~ * ~

Parker realized he couldn't concentrate on the ranch, work that usually cleared his mind no longer seemed as important as going back to the main complex. To be truthful, no one would fault him for his decision. He had too much on his mind to do his job with any efficiency.

Peter was waiting for him, when he returned. "I wondered how long you'd stay out there," he said.

Parker dismounted and turned to face his friend. "I just couldn't concentrate. Do you know if anyone has been able to prove that Warren was responsible for the deaths of my parents?"

"I haven't heard anything yet, but it's only been a few hours since we brought it up to Cassion and the others. These things take time, at least that's what everyone has been telling me. Why don't you go over to the dining hall? Connor usually has a pot of fresh coffee going for anyone who needs it."

"I think I need to talk to Jerilyn more than I need coffee. Do you think she will have time for me?"

"There's only one way to find out."

Peter activated his communicator and reached out to Jerilyn.

"Do you have some free time this afternoon?" he asked.

"I do. What's up?"

"Parker just rode in. He'd like to talk to you."

~ * ~

Jerilyn smiled at Peter's question. She'd been expecting to hear from Parker. The scuttlebutt was that Parker was harboring the same feelings for Sharday as she had for him. Considering Sharday was going to be here any minute, this might be the perfect time for the two of them to get together.

"I'm free now. Why don't you bring him over?"

Peter agreed and she prayed he would stay for the session. It would be good for Parker to have his friend with him for moral support.

It took only a few minutes for Peter and Parker to arrive, followed closely by Sharday. Jerilyn could tell by the look on Parker's face, he was wondering why she was also here.

"I-I didn't expect to see you here," Parker said as soon as Sharday entered the office.

"I could say the same about you."

"This joint session was my idea," Jerilyn interjected. "I have been watching the two of you and it's evident there are feelings growing between you. I can understand Parker's feelings as well as yours,

Sharday. The way I see it, Parker, you are enamored with Sharday but you feel inferior. After what happened in court yesterday, it's understandable. It was the same between Peter and me. I'd been rescued when I was the age of the girls who were brought here, therefore, I'd been educated at the Denver Complex. It took a while for Peter and me to connect and realize education had no relationship with love.

"Sharday, I've watched you since the day you arrived and I've seen the smile on your lips and in your eyes whenever you see Parker. You are worried that he will not think he's worthy of you or maybe the other way around. Someone has to intervene and get the two of you together. It might as well be me. True love can't be denied and sometimes it needs someone to make it happen."

She looked across the desk and noted the relief that showed on both Sharday and Parker's faces. At the time she set up the meeting, she worried about the prudence of her actions. Now she was positive she'd done the right thing.

"Is what Jerilyn said about you true?" Sharday asked.

Parker nodded his head. "The lawyer said it all yesterday when he called me a dumb cowpuncher. I don't have the education you do, but I'm working on getting it. I want you in my life and I pray to the One God that you want the same thing."

Sharday's smile said more than any words she would ever speak. "I've felt something special for you ever since I first came to the ranch. I didn't know what it was, but it was nothing I've ever felt before. My friend, Nova, tells me it's love. I don't know much about such things, but I think I've been in love with you for months. I'm dedicated to staying here and seeing to the needs of Betsy. From what I hear, you're dedicated to staying here and making this a safe haven for troubled youth. Would you be willing to carry on your work with me by your side?"

A low chuckle echoed from Parker's throat. "From what I've heard, I'm supposed to be the one asking that question. Fortunately, I love a forceful woman. If this crazy feeling I have every time I see you is love, then I love you. I might be just a dumb cowpuncher, but I'm working to change that. I think together we can do great things for Resurrection Ranch."

~ * ~

"Well, that went well, Miss Matchmaker," Peter said, once he and Jerilyn were alone in her office.

"I hoped it would. It was kinda like you and me. I was in love with you long before you ever looked my way. I didn't think you'd ever come around to realizing how much I cared for you."

"You're right. I had the same feelings as Parker. Even though I found a loving mother and step-father and was instantly independently wealthy, in reality I was much like Parker. I was little more than an ignorant cowpuncher. The difference being I was as comfortable wearing a suit and tie as I was in jeans and boots, riding the range. Realizing you loved me as much as I loved you was the greatest gift I could ever receive."

Chapter Sixteen

Cassion mulled over the information he'd received, regarding the murders of Parker, Dan and Betsy's parents. It was enough to make him sick. Each of the murders took place after the abducted children had been sold to either Henderson Ranch or Master.

"You look pensive," Hodia said. "What's going on?"

"Josie was right. Warren made certain the parents of these children were dead so no one could ever match them to family."

"Are they certain it was Warren who did the murders?"

"Not certain but the timelines all match up. When they arrested Master, they found he kept records as complete as the ones left by Henderson. It showed that three weeks after Betsy was abducted, her parents were killed. Just like the records kept by Henderson correspond with the timeline for the murders of Parker and Dan's families. I know it's circumstantial evidence, but it's evidence, nonetheless. I've won cases on less. According to the message I got this morning, I should be hearing from the police departments who first investigated the deaths. I promise I won't be jumping to any conclusions until I see the rest of the evidence."

"Well, my dear husband, for now, you won't be jumping into anything. I think you should turn this information as well as anything else you receive to the prosecution. They can take it from there. Once you do, I expect you back here for a nap."

"That's what I love about you, Hodia. You keep me grounded. It's hard for me to not want to be in the midst of this trial. You're right, I do need to rest and let others do the work."

~ * ~

Darien and Jason Culver read all the information Cassion gave to them. It was all eye opening to say the very least.

"How do you plan to implicate Warren in these murders?" Jason asked.

"When Warren was arrested, the police involved took custody of a large number of weapons. They're working to see if any of them were the ones used in the murder of Dan's mother as well as Betsy and Parker's parents."

"I thought Betsy and Parker's parents were killed in house fires."

"That was the official release, but they were killed before the fire started. There was no soot in any of their lungs. In other words, they were murdered. The fire was an attempt to disguise it as accidental. The pathology report said otherwise."

"I'm a bit rusty on things like ballistics, but how can you trace back to one of those laser pistols?"

"There are several people who prefer the old guns with bullets like the ones used in the twenty-first century. To be truthful, they are more accurate for long range shootings. Luckily, our friend Foster Warren was one of those people. The ballistics are being compared from all three local police forces involved in the murders of these people. We should have news on the results by tomorrow morning. I realize we've already delayed the trial by two days, but if we can link Warren to these murders, it will be worth it."

~ * ~

Parker heard the news about the murders of his parents as well as those of Betsy's parents, at dinner. It was the second day the trial had been delayed and everyone was questioning the delay.

"I can't believe my parents were killed before the fire was set," he said, when Jason gave him the news of what they'd learned. "Is there any way we can link the murders to Warren?"

"We're hoping so. He was using a regular pistol, rather than one of the new models of laser pistols. It, along with several other firearms, was confiscated when he was arrested. We won't know anything for certain until morning, but it looks like he could be behind at least five of the murders we're looking into."

Parker thanked Jason. As much as he wanted to think about what he just heard, he knew he had to talk to Sharday about the information he now had concerning the murder of Betsy's parents. He saw her sitting across the room and nodded to her before going to pick up his supper. By the time he was seated at the table with Sharday, he relaxed for the first time.

"I saw you talking to Officer Culver, did you learn anything new?" she asked.

"They were able to learn that my parents as well as Betsy's were murdered before the fires were started. It wasn't made public because at the time they had no gun to compare with the bullets used in the murders."

"Bullets, I don't understand."

"Jason told me some criminals prefer the old-fashioned weapons to the new laser models. In this case, there were several weapons confiscated when Warren was arrested. We won't know anything concrete until they are all tested, but it's a distinct possibility. At least it gives us a chance of convicting him of murder and sentencing him to life without parole."

Sharday wiped a tear from her eye. "It's a shame there is no longer a death penalty. I would love to either be on a firing squad or to at least be the one giving the lethal injection to end his miserable life. Betsy is having terrible night terrors about him being able to find her. I want it to end, for her sake as well as yours."

"I do too, but it all has to run its course. The way I see things, this is the best news we could have gotten."

"I tend to agree. Now, let's talk about something other than the trial."

"What did you have in mind?"

"How about those plans you have for Resurrection Ranch?"

"I have a better idea. How about plans for our future? I want to believe there will be a future for us when this is all over. I understand your need to remain close to Betsy, but I also have an obligation to finish my education. In the meantime, we can have a great time getting to know each other better."

Sharday nodded her agreement. He understood they came from two different worlds. Learning everything there was to know about each other would be a good thing to pass the time before they were both free of their obligations and ready to make a commitment to their future together as well as at Resurrection Ranch.

~ * ~

Sharday went back to her quarters and contacted her parents on her communicator. She was pleased to see both her mother and father's faces on the screen.

"How are you doing?" her mother asked.

"Good, now. I've met someone here."

"Someone from our people?" her father inquired.

"No, Dad. He's one of 'the Lost Boys' from the ranch."

"An Earthling?" both of her parents questioned in unison.

"Yes, an Earthling. He's a good man and he has great plans for the future of Resurrection Ranch. To be truthful, I want to be part of those plans as well as part of his life."

"Does he make you happy?" her father pressed.

"Happier than I've ever been in my life. For a while I worried that he wouldn't want to be part of my life, then I learned he worried that his lack of education made him inferior to me. We were both too stubborn to take the first step, but I'm so glad that my friend Jerilyn made us realize we needed each other."

"Does this young man have a name?" her mother asked.

"His name is Parker Flint. He lived a terrible life here as a child and was sold to one of the slave ranches in Mexico. He was even branded like an animal. I thank the One God every day that he was rescued and given a second chance at life. We both have obligations, me to my charge and he to his education. We are going to take the time we need to get to know each other until we are both free to marry and work for the future of the ranch."

"I am happy for you, daughter," her father said. "It sounds like we will have plenty of time to make arrangements to come to meet the young man who has made my daughter's eyes sparkle when she mentions his name."

With the information she'd dreaded sharing with her parents behind her, Sharday went on to elaborate on the trial that was being held and the new information she'd just learned from Parker.

"I don't understand how anyone could do such heinous things to children," her father commented.

In the background she could see her mother wiping tears from her eyes.

"These men were ruthless. They were working for the man who ran the ranch and abused the boys so badly. Considering everything they've been through; they are all adjusting well to their new lives as well as finishing the educations they were denied as children. I would love to have you visit and see what is being built here. It's an entirely different life than what we've known. I have to admit I am thrilled to be part of the project that is being built here."

The conversation turned to more mundane subjects, including information about Sharday's siblings and friends still living under Antarctica's ice cap.

By the time the conversation ended, it was well past the time when she should have been in bed. Going to the window of her room, she looked out at the full moon shining a silvery light over the entire compound. Glancing toward the boy's dorm, she wondered if Parker was looking out on the same moon and thinking of her as she was of him.

Chapter Seventeen

"We've got him," Darian declared as he burst into Jason's office. "The sheriff's department in Indiana was able to match the bullets from one of Warren's guns, it was a match to all five murders. There's no way he can get out of this one. We're lucky that bastard liked those old-fashioned weapons. Had he used a laser gun, there would be no way that we could have traced it back to him."

"That's the best news I've heard in a couple of days. Does Cassion know?"

"Not yet. I wanted to have you go over to his apartment with me to deliver the good news. I made an appointment with him for eight this morning before we resume the trial."

Together they went over to the apartment complex and took the elevator to the tenth floor. Hodia met them at the door.

"Cassion is anxious to meet with you. I hope you have good news to give him. He's been like a caged lion ever since he got the original reports."

"I know he wants to be part of this. That's why we're here so early this morning. He will want to be in court today."

"Are you talking about me?" Cassion asked, as he entered the sitting room.

"We are," Darian said. "We got back the ballistic report and three of Warren's old-fashioned weapons match the bullets used in all five murders. He must have thought no one would put two and two together to figure out the shooter in each of the murders was the same man because he used three different weapons."

Cassion breathed a sigh of relief. "It was worth collapsing and having to have the heart transplant to have been in on the capture of Warren. Does anyone else know about this?"

"Not yet. I'm planning to meet with Warren's attorney next to amend the charges to five counts of first-degree murder."

"Do you think Hammer and Constantine were also involved?"

"No. It seems they both had their own operation going. I could tell when we mentioned the murders, they had no idea just how rogue Warren went. I have a feeling neither of them ever contemplated anything so drastic."

~ * ~

Word went out throughout the compound, about the trial being resumed at eleven this morning. Once again, the Native American cowboys took over the duties usually done by the young men who wanted to be at the trial.

Parker and Sharday sat together, each wondering what today would bring as far as the trial was concerned.

The entire room was hushed as the three men on trial were brought to the defendant's table. Two days of being idle and not able to leave the locker room decreased their bravado from the first days of the trial.

"Your honor," Darian began, "at this point we would like to amend the charges against Forest Warren to include five counts of first-degree murder."

"Murder," Warren shouted as he got to his feet. "You have no proof."

The judge banged his gavel. "Restrain that defendant."

Once Warren was restrained, Darian continued. "We have concrete proof that the parents of Parker Flint and Betsy Potts were murdered with weapons owned by Warren before their homes were set on fire. We also have proof that the fly by shooting of Dan Campion's mother was done with another of Warren's weapons. Had he used laser weapons, it would have been harder to prove, but with the bullets from his guns they were a perfect match to the ones used in all five murders."

Although Parker expected this, he had no idea how hearing the actual accusations would affect him. He wanted to jump from his seat and attack Warren. He was ready to get to his feet when a wave of dizziness overwhelmed him. Only Sharday squeezing his hand kept him grounded.

He shook his head to rid himself of the dizziness, but it did little good. Instead, a cold sweat broke out on his forehead.

Before he could react, Dr. Petro was by his side. It took little in the way of persuasion for him to allow Dr. Petro to guide him to his feet and lead him from the courtroom. Once in the hallway, he gave into the dizziness and slipped into an unconscious state.

~ * ~

"Will he be alright?" Sharday asked, once she stepped out of the courtroom.

"I'm taking him over to the hospital. All of this has been very stressful for him. To hear the details of his parents' murder was too much for him. He will be sedated. I know you want to be with him, but he will expect you to remain in the courtroom, so you can advise him how things are going."

Reluctantly, she turned back once the orderlies took Parker to the hospital on one of the gurneys.

Chris, Mark, Peter and Clint all waited for her. As soon as she informed them about what Dr. Petro told her, they all took their seats and the trial began.

There was so much chatter going on throughout the room at the announcement of these new charges, the judge was forced to bang his gavel to regain order.

Once the room quieted down, he addressed the attorney representing Foster Warren. "What say you to these new charges leveled against your client?"

"Although my client wants to plead not guilty, the evidence is so damning, I feel it is best if he enters an Alfred plea."

The residents from Resurrection Ranch exchanged puzzled looks. None of them knew what an Alfred plea meant.

"Would you care to expand on the meaning of an Alfred plea?" the judge inquired.

"It is an antiquated plea in which a defendant maintains his innocence even though the prosecution has enough evidence against him to find him guilty."

Sharday was shocked that such a thing could be possible when no one had even heard of it before.

"Your plea is accepted. We will continue with the trial. Who do you call as your next witness, Darian?"

The prosecutor got to his feet. "I would like to call the ballistics expert from the sheriff's department in Indiana who performed the tests comparing the bullets from defendant's antiquated guns with those taken from the five victims. These murders were done so that if there was ever a chance of returning the children he kidnapped to their parents, it would be impossible. Our expert is Detective Quincy Barnett and he will be testifying via video from Indiana."

While everyone was still digesting what occurred since the beginning of this morning's segment of the trial, a large screen communicator was brought into the gym/courtroom.

~ * ~

"I honestly don't think this is necessary," Parker protested, when Dr. Petro insisted on a complete examination.

"I do. That's enough for you to know. Like everyone else on the ranch, you've been under a lot of stress during this trial. This morning's new evidence was extremely difficult for you to hear. Up until now, you have believed your parents' deaths were a terrible accident. It had to be traumatizing to realize they were murdered and the fire was started to cover up the crime. I've been watching all of the survivors of the atrocities that took place on this ranch. None of you have been eating enough and it is evident you aren't getting enough rest. Stress can do that to you. I would rather do an exam and find out things are normal for you than to have a repeat of this morning's weakness."

"You do make sense," Parker admitted. "My entire life has been stressful and this is bringing things to the forefront. Everything that happened to me after I was kidnapped, has been coming back to me and it wasn't pretty. Learning that my parents' deaths were murder rather than an accident put everything into perspective. Not only is the man a monster but he's also a murderer. I have a feeling he is responsible for more than the five murders for which he is now charged."

Dr. Petro nodded his head in agreement. "Unfortunately, we have no proof of any other murders he might have committed, just as we don't know how many other children he kidnapped. From what I've heard, my son-in-law has piles of files that no one has gone through. It is possible he brought children here who either died before they aged out or after they were sold to one of the ranches in Mexico as well as the hate groups in the Northwest area of the country."

Parker could feel tears threatening to spill from his eyes. He wondered how many other of the boys who were sold to Henderson, or the girls sold to the pimps, who had their parents murdered. Life wasn't fair and never had been for him. It was a miracle he'd survived long enough to be able to be rescued and returned to help rebuild Resurrection Ranch.

Rather than trying to argue further, Parker allowed Dr. Petro to do a complete physical scan. The result found anemia, stress and exhaustion. Against his better judgement, he agreed to let the doctor administer a mild sedative. His last thought before going to sleep was that his parents were already dead when the fire broke out sparing them the pains of dying from burns or smoke inhalation.

~ * ~

Sharday left the courtroom at the end of the day with more questions than answers. How could one person carry out such heinous crimes and still declare his innocence? She wondered if any of the three defendants would take the stand in their own defense. If any one of them did, how could they condone their behavior where the boys of Resurrection Ranch and her own charge, Betsy, were concerned.

Rather than going to the dining hall, she made her way to the hospital. Parker's collapse worried her, but she knew it was important for her to remain at the trial to represent not only Parker's interests but those of Betsy as well. She was loyal to both of them and needed to listen to the evidence against Foster Warren as well as the other two defendants.

At the hospital she saw Clint in conversation with Dr. Petro.

"What do you mean you had to hospitalize him?" She heard Clint say.

"I'm doing a complete physical. For that I need to have him hospitalized. As a matter of fact, I'd like to do the same for you and Peter as well as the children who were kidnapped by Forest Warren."

"If that's not the most asinine thing I've ever heard. We've all had complete physicals from Dr. Gratan. Isn't that enough?"

"In this case, no it's not. With the fact that Parker collapsed today, I began some of the testing. He is suffering from extreme stress as well as anemia. I have a feeling I will find the same thing with the rest of you. Having the men who kidnapped you on trial is stressful for everyone on the ranch. Hearing today's accusations about what happened to Parker, Betsy and Brad's parents, the stress level has risen one hundred percent. Even though your situation as well as Peter's are different, the stress of your lives has, most likely, taken a toll on each of you."

Sharday shuddered. She saw what happened to Parker earlier in the day. It upset her at the time, but she hadn't thought about what the realization about what happened to her parents would do to Betsy. Dan always knew his mother was murdered but knowing who did it might be detrimental to his wellbeing. He was just now beginning to overcome his learning disability and to adjust to life on the ranch where he'd been mistreated so badly. This could become a major setback in his road to recovery.

Turning her thought back to the conversation between Dr. Petro and Clint, she could tell something changed Clint's attitude.

"When you put it that way, Doc, I can see what you mean. Just seeing Noah Hammer again brought back some memories of when he kidnapped me from the foster home. I have been on edge ever since this damnable trial began. I'm anxious to get back to Mark's office and see how many more kids he sold to Henderson. So far, the only two I know of are Brad and myself. With all of the kids that went through this place, it's hard telling how much money he made selling kids off to this hellhole."

Even from her distance, she could see the tears that were running down Clint's cheeks. He was close to hysteria. Even though he hadn't had contact with the worst of the kidnappers, he'd been traumatized by what happened almost twenty years earlier.

All of the kids who passed through this place in the past were brought by men like these, they were in need of more than education. They would all need hours of counseling in order to put the past where it belonged. Watching Clint, told her his past was close to the surface. It was entirely possible he still had the nightmares she'd witnessed in Betsy since they realized Forest Warren was the man who kidnapped her and sent her to the pimp who wanted to train her to become a prostitute as soon as she was old enough.

At this point, she wished she was on the jury so she could beg for the death penalty. Of course, she knew it would be a mute issue since the death penalty had been abolished over seventy-five years ago all over the planet.

"Sharday," Dr. Petro said, breaking into her internal thoughts. "I didn't expect to see you here."

"I-I don't know why not. You must know that Parker and I have been seeing each other. I needed to check on him, but listening to the two of you, I think it's best if I get back to my charge, Betsy. I'm getting more and more worried about her wellbeing through all of this. I know she was physically and sexually abused by the man she calls Master. She has also told me what Warren did to her. Can I bring her over to the hospital so you can do a complete examination of her?"

"Of course, you can, but I think it would be best if my wife was the one to examine her. I have a feeling, she like the other girls would be more comfortable with a woman. The two men she's known in her life have, more than likely, traumatized her."

Sharday agreed. Even though she was concerned about Betsy, she knew it was best she not be further traumatized, if it could be helped.

~ * ~

"What did you make of this morning's proceedings?" Chris asked Mark.

135

"Every time I turn around, I find more and more atrocities about this place and the degenerates who supplied kids to Henderson. For you and me, things were different. We were sent here by well-meaning people. If it hadn't been for Jason, I don't know where I would have been sent. He asked for the social workers to do what they thought was best. As for you, it was the doctors at the hospital where you were born. In both cases they thought they were doing the best thing for us. No one had any idea what went on here, until you spilled the beans at the Denver complex. I don't blame Jason any more than you blame Dr. Parker. If anyone is to blame, it's the state of Nevada for funding this operation without making any inquiries about how it was run."

Chris slowly nodded his head. He knew Mark was right. The two of them were different from the other boys who were brought here. No one kidnapped them. They were sent to where people thought they would be well cared for because of the state funding.

"How many others do you think there are who were kidnapped?"

Mark motioned toward the row of file cabinets. "You know, we've only scratched the surface. There are years of files that we haven't even looked at. What little we've uncovered is just the tip of the iceberg. It's a blessing that after this trial is over, all three of them will be put away where they can never do these things to another child. Do you think they will be sent to the dark side of the moon or under the ice cap of Antarctica?"

"It's hard telling. Something tells me they won't be sent to the same facility. I've heard talk about an asteroid that's close to the moon has been colonized and made habitable for a penal colony. Due to all the crime that has been uncovered on earth lately, they feel it is necessary for the worst of the worst. It doesn't matter where they go. What does matter is that they are off the face of the earth. What I worry about is how we can make this ranch work, not only for us but for other troubled youth in the future."

The buzzing of Mark's communicator broke up their conversation. It had no sooner buzzed, than Chris' communicator did as well.

"Clint?" Mark questioned when his friend's face filled the screen.

"I hope you don't mind me making this a conference call with you, me and Chris."

"Of course, I don't mind. We are both in the office together. What's going on?"

"Dr. Petro hospitalized Parker and he wants to do the same for Dan, Betsy and me. He says he's worried about the stress of this trial. I was mad at first then I realized it was for the best. This trial has been hard on all of us. It's been harder on Parker because of what we learned about his parents' deaths. Luckily, it manifested itself when he collapsed at the trial this morning. I agreed and I'm being admitted to the hospital this afternoon. I know it leaves us shorthanded, but if there is something wrong with us…"

"I totally agree," Chris interrupted. "We need everyone to be in the best shape possible if we're going to bring our dreams for this place to fruition. We'll finish up here and be over to the hospital to check on both of you. In the meantime, we'll contact Felton and Sharday to bring their charges over as well."

"Sharday was here when Dr. Petro and I were talking about this. I don't know about Felton, but Sharday went back to the trailer she shares with Betsy to bring her to the hospital. One thing that Dr. Petro did say was that they've been doing research on stress on the dark side of the moon, mostly on the people who have been sent to the penal colony there. Since many of them are from Earth, they are learning more about earthly stress, since the lives of the aliens on the moon are relatively stress free."

"Interesting," Chris mused. "Perhaps we should bring Peter with us. Even though this trial doesn't apply to him, he could be having the same problems because of Delos Reynolds. If Peter's father hadn't killed the man, it's quite possible he would have been on trial with the rest of them."

~ * ~

Peter was surprised when he returned to the ranch at the end of the day to find Mark and Chris waiting for him.

"What's up?" he asked.

He realized something must have happened at the trial today. Not being there he wondered if something was terribly wrong. Had the three defendants somehow managed to escape. Were the residents of Resurrection Ranch in danger?

"Parker collapsed at the trial today," Mark said. "He's been hospitalized for a complete physical and mental examination. Dr. Petro has asked that the rest of us submit to the same exams."

"I don't understand. I wasn't kidnapped by any of the men on trial."

"You were kidnapped," Chris replied. "You've been through the stress of the trial for your father and the horrors of learning he was a serial killer. Mark and I are going to have the exam and so are the older guys. It's nothing more than a precaution, but Dr. Petro says they are doing research of earthly stress on the inmates of the penal colony. They've made great strides that haven't been brought to Earth yet."

"I can see what you mean. I think it's a good idea. No matter how any of us got here, we've all been under a lot of stress ever since we first were brought here. I saw my father prosecuted for his crimes, but that didn't erase everything I endured. I'm willing, whenever Dr. Petro is ready for me."

"I understand what you're saying. You weren't at the trial for the Henderson's, like Mark and I were. That was a rough one, but so was the one for the Grainger's. As I recall that's where I first met you. Both of those couples took a lot away from us, including our ability to handle stress. I'm Glad Dr. Petro is here to help us deal with that kind of stuff."

Peter made his way to the dining hall, where Jerilyn waited for him. He knew he needed to talk to her about what was going on, especially the possibility of being hospitalized for stress. With her background in therapy, she would be able to help him put everything into perspective.

Chapter Eighteen

"Josie, Josie Rawlins, is that you?"

Josie turned to see Brendon McDougal hurrying to catch up with her. She cringed, realizing he was the last person she wanted to see on Resurrection Ranch. Immediately, she recalled the night he took her to the prom when they were in high school. His father was among the high echelon of Maquoketa society. Brendon was someone her father approved of to take her out. For her it was a horrible night. Brendon was extremely self-centered and even suggested they go to a secluded spot where they could have sex. Like that was ever going to happen.

"Brandon, what are you doing here?"

"I was going to ask you the same question. I thought you would be as far away from here as possible, after that mess with your father."

"I'm here because I want to be part of this ranch. I'm teaching not only the children but also the adults who were denied an education. That doesn't answer my question. Why are you here?"

"I'm working for the Free Press out of Des Moines. They sent me down to cover the trial, especially after what information came out yesterday about Foster Warren killing all those people and abusing those children. What do you say you come to my hotel in town and we pick up where we left off on prom night?"

I'd rather kiss a snake. "That wouldn't be possible. I'm going to be late for my class. Like I said, I have a job here teaching. I take my responsibilities very seriously."

"Class? This late at night?"

"Yes, this late at night. The adults who are taking classes from me work on the range during the day. The only time they can have their classes is at night."

"Adults? Don't you mean illiterate cowboys?"

With all the control she could muster she refused to reach out to

139

slap Brendon's face. "That's where you're wrong. They were denied an education when they were children and have progressed extremely quickly. They are far from illiterate. In fact, they are highly intelligent. Some of them are already preparing for college educations. We are in the process of building a college on the property and looking to find the proper professors in order to be able to cater to whatever needs they might have. We are already working on a veterinary program for those who are interested in following that vocation. Now if you will excuse me, I must be going."

To her surprise, Brendon grabbed her arm. "What about Zander? Is he here, too? I'd like to see him. It might make for a good interview for the paper. From what I hear, he's guilty of several crimes against this ranch. Is he in prison?"

"I think that's something you should talk to him about. As a matter of fact, he's coming our way right now."

Brendon turned to see Zander approaching from the dining hall. "Zander," he called. "Do you remember me?"

Josie was relieved to be able to get away from Brendon's unwanted attentions. She hated shoving him off on Zander, but hurried toward the education complex. The thought of seeing Clint there tonight, made her feel much better.

By the time she entered the classroom, she saw Clint sitting by himself. With everything that was going on, could she do justice to tonight's class? She was certain he'd heard about Parker's collapse earlier in the day and wondered how it would affect him.

"You look like I feel," Clint greeted her. "Who gut punched you?"

"Someone from my past, Brendon McDougal, is here to cover the trial for a paper in Des Moines. He was my prom date from hell."

"Prom?"

She was sorry she'd said that. Proms were things that only happened in small towns where people didn't like to let go of old traditions. From what she learned in college; the big cities no longer participated in such archaic practices.

"The prom is a dance that is held in small towns at the end the student's senior year in high school. The girls wear formal dresses and the boys wear fancy suits. It's a big deal, although I was never thrilled about going."

"Why not?"

"Because my dad pushed Brendon's father to get him to take me. I didn't like him in high school and I like him less now. He is so full of himself he even asked me to go to his hotel so he could finish what he couldn't start on prom night."

"Are you saying he wanted to…?"

Josie nodded, not wanting to hear Clint say the word rape or think that she hadn't kept herself pure throughout her life.

"Where is he?"

"It doesn't matter. I sicked him onto Zander. I think we should get started on tonight's lesson."

"I'd rather have you show me how to dance. I've heard about it but I've never done it. Since Parker isn't here tonight, that way he wouldn't be getting behind in our studies."

Without music playing in the background, she showed him how to hold her and began to show him the steps of the dances she participated in at the prom.

"It's much better with music," she said, once he held her in his arms and practiced the steps, she'd taught him.

"I'm sure it is, but I do enjoy holding you like this. I heard that Mark's sister is having dance classes for the little kids. Maybe she can incorporate that into our lesson plans. So many of us have found special people in our lives, maybe we can have our own prom."

She had to admit she liked Clint's idea, but she liked being alone with him like this. The way he held her in his arms, made her melt like butter. She'd been on many dates, but no one ever made her feel like she did when she was with Clint. Of course, her other dates had all been guys like Brendon, because her father approved of them. In no way would he ever approve of Clint.

It was late when the class period ended. Even though she wanted to keep dancing, she knew they needed to do some academic work as well. With Parker in the hospital, she was able to work one on one with Clint and cover the information she'd prepared for tonight's class in record time.

"May I walk you home?" Clint asked, as they left education center.

"I would like that."

As soon as they left the building, she saw Brendon waiting for her.

"Is your class over?" he asked.

"Yes, it is."

"Good, would you like to come into town with me for either dessert or a drink?"

Josie felt Clint tighten his grip on her hand. "I'm sorry, I can't make it. I usually avoid dessert and I don't drink."

"I could think of something else to do."

"Did you hear the lady?" Clint inquired. "She said she can't make it. Now, I'm going to make certain she gets back to her apartment safely."

Brendon stood in their way. "So, that's the way it is. Are you planning to spend the night with the lovely Miss Rawlins?"

"Hardly. Once I make certain she's safely to her door, I will be going to the dorm. I have homework to finish before I go to bed and five o'clock comes mighty early in the morning. I do have a full day of work to accomplish before my lesson tomorrow night."

"Are you telling me you want a dumb cowboy over someone like me?" Brendon spat; his question directed at her.

"I would much rather spend my time with someone of my choosing rather than someone my father bribed to take me to the prom. Have a good night, Brendon. I for one am ready for bed, alone."

Clint took her arm and pushed their way past an astonished Brendon.

~ * ~

Zander never understood why Josie was such a twit about having to go to prom with Brendon. After talking to him for five minutes, he no longer doubted why she didn't want to go with him.

Within the first five minutes of their conversation, the man showed himself to be completely self-centered. After telling Zander about

142

his many successes, he finally asked why he wasn't in prison for the attack on Resurrection Ranch.

Talking about the part he'd played in his father's plan to destroy everything here made him sick to his stomach. He'd been pleased to be able to tell Brendon of the treatment he'd been granted both at the hospital as well as by the people who were the heart and soul of this ranch. He ended by explaining about his sentence of five years working on the ranch and getting an education at the same time.

"Why would you need an education? You weren't brought up here?" Brendon asked.

It brought a lump to Zander's throat to have to tell this pompous ass how his father denied him the chance for a college education, insisting he should be content to work in the insurance office. Now that he had a chance to do something that interested him more than insurance, he could see a bright future opening up when his five years of work on the ranch was finished.

In the distance, he saw Clint walking Josie back to the apartment complex. He waited until they got closer before he stepped out of the shadows.

"I like the way you handled our old friend, Clint," Zander said.

"I should have decked him. He gave me the creeps to say nothing of the effect he had on Josie."

"I know what you mean. I thought he was a pretty great guy when he was on the varsity football team in his freshman year. I was older but I still followed the high school football team. Never went to college, so didn't get into the college ball. After tonight, I've changed my mind. I've never met anyone with such a dirty mind in my life. In about fifteen minutes, he told me about at least ten of his conquests, as he called them. Girls he took to bed just to take their virginity. It made me sick to my stomach."

Josie nodded her head. "He propositioned me twice tonight. I think it bothers him that I didn't want any part of his advances when I was in high school. I was certainly pleased to have Clint with me when he cornered me as I came out of the educational center."

"The way it sounds, sis, is that he's going to be around for the next few days. He thought he was going to get to interview our dad. When I told him that Pops had been transferred to a medical hospital for the criminally insane, I could tell he was disappointed. I talked to Mark and we both decided that until he goes back to Iowa, you aren't going to be alone. In no way does he need any opportunity to get you alone. I know what he has on his mind and he's not going to do anything like that to my sister."

"What about the other women on the ranch?" Clint asked.

"Mark and Chris have agreed about no one being alone around him. As soon as this damnable trial is over, he'll be gone."

Zander no more than spoke the words, when a siren sounded, alerting everyone to an emergency in the area of the gymnasium where the trial was being held. People ran from every direction in order to get to the gym to see what was happening.

~ * ~

Mark and Peter were the first to arrive at the gym. From behind the locked door of the locker room, sounds emanated that sounded like a knock down drag them out fight.

"What's going on?" Mark asked the guard who was posted out of the door.

"I haven't opened the door," the guard replied. "I just heard what sounded like a fight and hit the alarm. I didn't want to get into the middle of anything by myself."

"Unlock the door," Peter requested.

As soon as the door opened, the sight of Foster Warren's badly beaten body was enough to turn anyone's stomach.

"What happened here?" Mark demanded.

"I beat the shit out of the bastard," Noah said. "After what we heard in court this morning, he couldn't stop bragging about what he did to not only those kids, but also to their parents. I thought I knew him but he's not the same person I grew up with. I know I kidnapped kids who ended up with Henderson, but I never did any of the things he did. I don't believe in anything like that. I probably would have killed him, if you hadn't opened that door. It's what he deserves."

"That wouldn't make you any different from him," Peter commented. "Do you realize you'd be charged with murder?"

"I do. It doesn't matter much. I'm going to be sent to one of the penal colonies for the rest of my life, and it's what I deserve. There's no death penalty, so one way or another I'm going to be punished."

Others began arriving along with orderlies from the hospital. Mark wondered how they knew to bring a gurney. Someone must have contacted them. Perhaps it was the guard who let them into the room.

As the orderlies lifted Foster to the gurney, Mark could hear him groan. At least he wasn't dead. Of course, after what they'd learned in court this morning, it was a shame he was still alive.

Jason Culver arrived and asked the same questions of Noah and Jasper. The story remained the same.

"What do you make of this, Mark?" Jason asked, once the door was again locked.

"I tend to agree with Noah. It's a shame he didn't kill the bastard. What he did to those kids he took, to say nothing of their parents, is an atrocity. It's hard telling how many other people suffered at his hand. I'm afraid we've only scratched the surface. Someone like that shouldn't be allowed to walk on the face of Earth."

"You make sense," Jason agreed. "Unfortunately, in a civilized world, we can't take the law into our own hands."

"Civilized world," Peter spat. "Like hell this was ever a civilized world for us. I didn't suffer at Warren's hands, I did suffer what Henderson did to us, to say nothing about what we endured either on those slave ranches or with the skin heads. In our world survival came at the cost of many of our friends. So, don't talk to me about civilized worlds."

Mark realized that although he'd been sent to Henderson Ranch by well-meaning social workers, it wasn't the same with everyone else he'd grown up with. It was no wonder Dr. Petro wanted each of them to undergo complete exams to deal with the stress they'd been living under all of their lives.

Chapter Nineteen

News of the attack on Foster Warren spread like a prairie fire during a drought. Even the personnel at the hospital were talking about it.

Parker heard bits and snatches from his hospital bed and was anxious to learn exactly what was going on. When he asked the nurses, his request was met with silence. He decided it must be because they weren't allowed to discuss details about their patients.

"I just talked to Dr. Petro," Mark said when he entered Parker's room. "He told me you're going to be released today and has given you a plan for further treatment."

"I know. I'm ready to get out of here and be able to know what's going on. What happened to Foster last night?"

The look on Mark's face told him his friend wasn't comfortable talking about the events of the previous evening.

After a short pause, Mark related the events that landed Foster Warren in a coma in the intensive care ward.

"I wish I would have been the one who did it to him," Parker said, after taking a moment to digest all of the details of the beating Warren suffered.

"No, you don't. Hammer has nothing to lose. He knows where the trial is heading. He'll be going to one of the penal colonies for the rest of his life. You, on the other hand, have everything to lose. The future of this ranch rests on all of our shoulders. We've been through hell, but we're getting a second chance at life. This isn't the time to blow it."

Parker nodded. "You're right, of course. After what he did to my parents as well as those of the other kids, makes me sick to my stomach. If we're all lucky, he won't regain consciousness. He's better off dead than mooching off the system for the rest of his life. If he's in as bad a shape as it sounds, he won't have to do any of the hard labor that he deserves."

The expression on Mark's face told Parker he agreed.

"So, I doubt this is a social call," Parker continued. "Are you here to spring me out of this joint?"

"I am. According to Dr. Petro, the best thing for you is to get your butt on a horse and get back to work. The trial for the other two defendants is going to continue, but until we know more about Warren's condition, the remainder of his trial will be on hold. We all know he's as guilty as sin, but since he's in a coma, we cannot continue. At least that's what Darien told the judge at the court this morning before the beginning of today's proceedings."

~ * ~

Clint watched as Noah Hammer and Jasper Constantine were ushered into the makeshift courtroom. It was evident Noah had been in a fight and perhaps got as good as he gave. His left eye was swollen shut and his corresponding cheek was stitched shut and badly bruised.

To everyone's surprise, the lawyer representing Noah got to his feet before anyone else could get up to speak.

"My client would like to address the court, against my advice."

"Are you certain about this, Mr. Hammer?" the judge asked.

"I am, your honor. I'm not as smart as the average guy, but I do know the things I did for Jasper and Henderson are wrong. Why should I go on with this travesty of a trial? I'm guilty, just as I'm guilty of the beating I gave to Warren last night. I want this nightmare to be over. My life is over. Sentence me and end the rest of it now. Whatever you sentence me to is exactly what I deserve. There is no reason to prolong this any longer. I kidnapped those boys from the foster homes, because it was what Jasper asked me to do. I never molested them, like Warren did and I never touched girls. Is there anything more you want me to tell you?"

"I think that is sufficient. In light of what you have told the court, I sentence you to imprisonment on the dark side of the moon for no less than ten years and no more than your natural life. Your sentence will begin immediately at a secure facility here on Earth, until the next shuttle to the moon arrives. In light of your confession, should you show good behavior, you may be able to be released earlier, rather than fulfilling your entire sentence. I will also recommend you be put into a program to help you learn how to be a productive citizen of this planet."

Clint felt a lump begin to grow in his stomach and threaten to force him to vomit what he'd eaten at the dining hall for breakfast. He doubted if Hammer would ever become a productive citizen, but anything was possible.

He watched as one of the guards attached electronic cuffs to his wrists and led him from the courtroom. Before he left the courtroom, Clint saw him turn to make eye contact. Noah stopped for a moment and turned toward Clint.

"I'm sorry for what I did to you. I knew what Henderson was doing, but the money was good. Jasper was my boss and he told me it was part of my job. I did what I was told and profited from it in the same way as the others did. I hope you can make your life something to be proud of. I know I'm not proud of mine."

Clint couldn't get any words past the lump in his throat. Instead, he nodded his head in agreement with what Noah just told him. In a way he pitied the man. He admitted he wasn't smart. Between Henderson and Constantine, he'd been led into a life of crime. Even though the punishment fit the crime, he wondered how Noah would survive in the isolation of the dark side of the moon.

I need to talk to you. Meet me at the office before we go to the dining hall for lunch. – Mark

Chris wondered what the urgency was for Mark's message. Without even telling anyone where he was going, he left his office and hurried across the common area of the compound.

"What's so urgent?" Chris asked as he entered Mark's office.

"This morning, I was able to go through some of the older files and I found this."

Mark handed the file to Chris so he could read the contents. What it held, came as a shock. All along, they'd known that Jasper Constantine was making money off of the boys who were taken to the ranch by Noah Hammer. What this file contained, was further damning evidence.

It seemed that Jasper was older than Noah and the others who participated in taking unsuspecting boys to the ranch. From what the ranch was when they were children, was a far cry from what it became. To his amazement, the entire plan had been organized and set in motion by Jasper under a company by the name of Ranchers, Inc. In addition to the money that graced Jasper's bank account, money was paid on a monthly basis to Ranchers, Inc. Of course, the company was little more than a shell and the money went to Jasper.

"That old bastard," Chris spat. "He set this whole thing up and defrauded Henderson of more money than he actually deserved. Have you shared this with Darien?"

"Not yet. Court is still in session. I've been monitoring it and Hammer confessed to everything, even the beating of Warren last night. He just wanted the trial over and volunteered to whatever sentence he was given. He was sentenced to no less than ten years and no more than his natural life in the penal colony on the dark side of the moon. Before he was taken away in electronic cuffs, he made eye contact with Clint and apologized to him. From what I could see, it was a very moving moment."

"I'm sure it must have been. It sounds like Hammer was little more than a pawn in Jasper's evil plan. How much money must he have made off the kids he was instructed to bring here?"

"A lot. From the log I found this morning, it was well over a billion dollars. As soon as I turn it over to Darien, it will certainly seal his fate. There will be no minimum sentence for him to serve. This afternoon's session should be quite interesting to say the very least."

~ * ~

"It sounds like there was quite a shock in court this morning," Chris said, when Clint entered the dining hall for the noon meal.

"It was. I have no desire to go back for any more of the trial. It wasn't until Hammer stopped and apologized to me, that I realized he was little more than a pawn for Henderson and Constantine. He did what they wanted without thinking he was hurting anyone because the kids were all in foster care with no one to care what happened to them."

"I can understand what you're saying," Chris commented. "I was sent here because the social workers at the hospital thought they were doing the right thing. It was the same with Mark. Until we came forward, no one knew what was going on here. Now it's our job to make changes that will help kids in the future rather than make things worse for them."

Chris watched as Clint went to join Josie and Zander at a table on the far side of the room. He thought about what Clint told him. Hammer, like the man who brought Peter to Henderson Ranch, was not smart enough to see anything beyond the money Henderson gave to them. It was a shame that Henderson changed so many lives in his quest for free labor and a large bank account.

"You didn't tell him about what we found out concerning Constantine. Why not?"

"I didn't think I was the proper person to tell him. Let it come out in court this afternoon. I know he doesn't want to go back, but between the two of us, we have to find a way to get him to go there with us this afternoon."

Mark took a moment to digest what Chris said. "You're right. We'll talk to him once we finish eating."

~ * ~

Josie was relieved when she saw Clint enter the dining hall. She'd heard all the gossip about what happened last night to Foster Warren and this morning in the courtroom. It all made her concern for Clint more profound. He was as fragile as Parker where this trial was concerned. They'd lived through the same horrors because of the men on trial and would do so for the rest of their lives.

"How are you doing?" Zander asked before Josie could ask the same question.

"I can't lie, this morning was rough. I'm beginning to see Hammer in a different light. He now understands what he did was wrong, including last night's beating of Warren. He's ready to serve his sentence."

"I heard they were sending him to the dark side of the moon as soon as a shuttle is available," Josie said. "At least there he might get some help toward rehabilitation."

She knew the words she spoke were little more than a hopeful wish. No one knew what went on in those penal colonies, but she doubted if any of it was rehabilitation. From what she'd heard, hard labor was the prescribed punishment for the prisoners who were sent there.

"Has your friend contacted you again?" Clint asked, changing the subject. "I saw him at the trial this morning."

"I haven't heard anything from him, but I don't put anything past him."

"At the time Pops suggested he take you to prom, I thought he was a great catch. After talking to him last night, I'm not so sure. Did you know the old man paid for all of the prom expenses for him?"

Josie looked at Zander. "Why in the world would he do that?"

"Apparently, he owed Brendon's father for some favor he'd done him. He'd been told that Brendon wanted to ask you out, but you wouldn't give him the time of day."

"You know why. I wasn't even planning on going to the prom. It was Dad who told me I was going and who I was going with. It was easier to do what he said than to…"

Tears cut off her last words. In the past she'd never told anyone about the things her father did to her has punishment. He hadn't gone as far as to attack her sexually. The mental and physical abuse had been enough to keep her in line. He knew how to cause pain without leaving marks. It was their secret, at least that was what he told her.

"Don't cry," Clint prompted. "We all know your father was mentally ill and he's where he can't hurt anyone ever again."

"I know," she said, wiping the tears from her eyes. "I honestly never told anyone about what he did. He had ways of tormenting me that didn't leave any marks."

From the look on Zander's face, she could tell he understood exactly what she was talking about.

All conversation ceased, when Dr. Petro entered the room. "I have an announcement to make. Foster Warren passed away from his injuries at ten this morning. I have advised his brother. I realize it's not the outcome most of you were hoping for, but his injuries were too extensive to save his life."

~ * ~

"I thought I told you I don't ever want to go back to that courtroom again," Clint protested.

"You did," Chris agreed. "Mark discovered some additional information this morning. We both agree it's something you should hear."

"What should I hear?"

"Chris is right, you should hear it, but not from us," Mark agreed. "We've turned over some evidence to the prosecution, that will change everything."

Clint was puzzled, but didn't say anything more. Instead, he agreed to accompany Mark and Chris to the afternoon session of the proceedings against now only one defendant.

"Is there anything you would like to say to the court, Mr. Constantine?" the judge asked.

"Yes, your honor," Jasper said, getting to his feet. "This trial, at least for me, is a sham. I didn't not procure any of the boys who were brought to this ranch."

"I object, your honor," Darien declared. "We have discovered new information that we would like to present to the court, outlining the extent of the defendant's involvement with the atrocities that were being carried out on this ranch. We have also contacted Theodore Henderson to see if he corroborates this information. I have his taped testimony for the court to listen to."

The judge agreed and Darien sat up a computer, so everyone in the room could hear the testimony.

"My name is Theodore Henderson. For many years, I ran Henderson Ranch under the guidelines of Ranchers, Inc. It was Jasper Constantine who introduced me to the company and their rules and regulations for running an operation such as ours. I agree that Jasper was compensated for the kids he sent here with Noah Hammer. I also sent compensation to Ranchers, Inc. Until today, I had no idea that no such company exists. It was nothing more than a sham company, set up by Jasper to satisfy his greed."

Clint looked over to where Jasper was sitting. As the taped message ended, he could see the color completely drain from Jasper's face.

"What do you have to say to this new evidence?" the judge asked.

Jasper sat mute, merely shaking his head.

"In light of this new evidence, I will give your lawyer time to confer with you as to how you want to proceed."

"It-it's all…" Jasper tried to get to his feet, but clutched his chest and slumped back to his chair.

In no time at all, medical personnel arrived. After administrating CPR for fifteen minutes, they pronounced Jasper dead of a massive heart attack.

Clint watched everything that was going on in disbelief. From the looks on Chris and Mark's faces he knew they felt the same way.

"H-How did you know the company was a scam?" Clint finally asked Mark.

"When I found the information, I looked up the company on the Internet. There was only one person listed as the CEO and President of the company and that was Jasper Constantine. The only ranch sending money to the company was Henderson Ranch. There will have to be a lot more searching for other information about where the money that was sent in for so many years. It should be interesting to find out where he has the proceeds from this bogus company stashed."

Chapter Twenty

It took several weeks for the effects of the trial of the three men who procured boys for Henderson Ranch to become almost ancient history. With those responsible for the kidnappings either dead or in secure facilities, it was time for the residents of Resurrection Ranch to begin the healing process.

"I've got some news to share with everyone," Cassion announced, one night at supper. "As you know, we have been looking into the money that was sent to Ranchers, Inc. We have finally found it, and the courts have decided the best use for it is to give it to Resurrection Ranch. The total amount that was found is well in excess of a billion dollars. I have talked to our financial advisors and they have suggested we invest the money and use only the interest for several years. Our investment will grow and we will be financially secure for several years, until we begin making money from our cattle and horses." The gathered crowd cheered. With the stability of the money recovered from Ranchers, Inc. The future of Resurrection Ranch was secure. They would be able to recover from their own experiences and bring a bright future to young men and women who would be coming to them in the future.

Epilogue

Five years passed and to everyone's delight Resurrection Ranch prospered. After many talks with the state, they qualified as a home for troubled youth, both male and female.

All the original 'Lost Boys' found love and acceptance. In a short period of time, the older students progressed through their elementary and secondary classes. They were each ready to begin their college educations at the beginning of the fall term.

The ranch teemed with life. The 'Lost Boys' were becoming parents and learning the proper way to raise their children.

With each passing year, the state of Nevada as well as other states, were sending troubled youth to the facility. At first the adjustment to the facility had been difficult. With each new set of young men and women, the routine was established. The young people who came to them were angry at being sent there. It usually took about a month for them to accept what was being offered to them was something they couldn't have gotten either living at home or on the streets.

"Can you believe what we've built here?" Chris asked, as he and Mark stopped their horses at the top of a hill overlooking Resurrection Ranch.

"Life has been good for all of us. We couldn't ask for anyone any better than Peter to handle the promotion of what we are doing here. He's the perfect poster boy for Resurrection Ranch."

"The future does look good for us. I hope these kids can benefit from what we are offering them. I see most of them through the educational system. Some of them are happy here and eager to learn. Others are belligerent, just as Brad was when he first got here. They're turning around, but it is a slow process."

"In a few weeks I'll be giving up the management of the ranch to start training with my uncle to become a veterinarian. Clint is taking over for me until my sister is ready to handle the position."

"I heard. I think that is the perfect solution. I'm lucky that I can maintain my position while I continue to pursue my education."

In the distance a hawk swooped down on its intended prey. From the Native American cowboys who continued to work at the ranch, Chris knew this was a good sign. Resurrection Ranch was alive and well. So much so that even the wild animals returned to the area to give their approval of the resurrection of the ranch and the land from evil to good.

Coming December 1, 2022
by the Author
at
Rogue Phoenix Press

Umba
The Secrets Series Book Three

CHAPTER ONE
UMBA DIG – KENYA – 2036

A cool predawn breeze kissed Leonore's cheek as she prepared for her morning run. She'd been in Kenya, working on the UMBA archaeological dig, for three weeks now and wondered why she'd come to Africa in the first place.

When she received her acceptance letter on this dig, she thought she could make a difference here. Instead, she found herself the only female volunteer. Dr. Conrad Kaufman had been furious when he realized Leo was short for Leonore. Although she signed her letter of application as Leonore P. Hayes, her letters of recommendations from friends and professors all called her Leo.

If it weren't for the fact, she needed this summer on UMBA for her post graduate course at Hamelin in the fall, she'd chuck the whole thing and go back to the states. Surely Dr. Grant-Clark would understand. Perhaps she would even allow her to take this year's course and do her field work on another dig next summer.

She shook her head to clear her mind, and started her morning run. Putting off thee run any longer would make her late for breakfast.

As usual, when she ran, she saw few animals. The drought caused them to migrate to other area in search of water. At least that's what she'd been told by a man she met occasionally when she went running.

She enjoying talking to the man who called himself *The Nomad*. Although he didn't look like the other natives of Kenya she'd met, he told her he'd lived most of his life in the area. She judged him to be in his late forties, but the way he spoke reminded her of an older, wiser man. Maybe it was his golden-brown skin, dark eyes and dark hair, which made her think him to be younger.

Without warning, the earth beneath her feet gave way. She grasped at the dry grass. For a moment, it stopped her sudden fall, then it gave way sending her tumbling the last few feet to the bottom.

Leo felt the air expel from her lungs from the force of the landing on smooth stones. After taking inventory of her body parts, she deducted there was nothing broken. Sitting up she reach for the flashlight strapped to her waist.

The beam illuminated the cavern. She gasped in disbelief. Before her stood an altar table, with trappings much like the ones she read about. Searching her memory, the words *Round Tree*, in West Virginia unfurled. Afraid to touch anything, she flashed the light around, allowing it to fall on stone jars and statues coated with a strange purple substance.

"My god," she said aloud. "What is this place?"

She received no answer to her question. In reality, she needed no answers. She knew them already. Twenty-five years earlier, Round Tree had been called the find of the century. If her assumptions were correct, she, Leo Hayes, just made a find that would be every bit as important to Africa as Round Tree was to America.

~ * ~

New Hope Mission – Kenya – 2028

David Clark woke in the guesthouse where he'd lived for the past two years. At noon the mission's helicopter would take him to Nairobi to the airport for his flight to London. He would stay there for a week, visiting his twin sister, Chris, and her husband, Neal, before going back to Roundtree and his parents.

He wondered how his dad would take the news about him not going back to school to get his doctorate in anthropology. Two years ago, he applied for a position with the Christian mission in Kenya. He wanted to take the two-year assignment to get his head together and decide what to do with the rest of his life.

Growing up, being shuttled between Round Tree and Havelin College threw his life into turmoil. He knew the ins and outs of archaeology, perhaps better than most people. His father, Dr. Evan Clark, would surely expect him to go back to school, get his doctorate, then join his half-brother at Round Tree.

His mother, Dr. Jocelyn Grant-Clark, on the other hand would understand his decision to teach history. When he returned to the states, he planned to start sending out resumes. Some district must want someone with his background and equalizations. With the world fighting back after the pandemic that struck eight years earlier, teachers were in high demand.

A knock at the door interrupted his thoughts. "David, are you awake?" Jeff Farnsworth, the head of the mission project called. "You have an oversees phone call."

David set aside his musings and pulled on a pair of khaki shorts before opening the door. "Who'd be calling me?" he asked.

"He said he's your dad. It's funny, I've rarely heard you speak of your family."

David didn't comment. His stomach did cartwheels as he crossed the compound to the main house that doubled as the office. In the entire time he'd been in Africa, there had been e-mails and an occasional letter from home, never a phone call.

"Dad?" David questioned, putting the receiver to his ear. "Is something wrong?"

"It's not what you think," his father began. "Everyone is all right. In fact, your mother and Brandon are here with me. We have you on speaker phone."

David checked his watch. It read eight-thirty, which would make it two-thirty in the morning back home. "Since I'll be home in about a week, I can't believe this is a social call. What's up?"

Dad got an e-mail from Kenya yesterday," Brandon interjected. "It seems Dr. Conrad Kaufman has a dig out there. He claims to have found a parallel society to Round Tree."

"A dig? Out here? I haven't heard of any. What's it called?"

"He referred to it as UMBA," Evan said. "He says he's about ten ours out of Nairobi by land. He's been there for about a year, unearthing a small village. I told him not to do anything until we could get someone there to authenticate it."

David's mind spun. Instead of flying out to London tomorrow, he would be meeting either his parents or his brother at the Nairobi airport/ "What time does your fight get in? I'll change my flight and meet you."

From the other side of the Atlantic, there was a moment of silence. "Look, Dave," Brandon finally added. "No one can get away. It's the twenty-fifth anniversary of the findings here. We're crazy with tourists, especially since the aired that old movie about Jaycee and Dad a couple of weeks ago."

David knew what Brandon meant. Even in this remote part of Kenya, they'd aired the movie on the International Network. He'd watched it with Jeff. Seeing it, made him a homesick.

"We know you're anxious to get home," his mother said, speaking for the first time. "We also know it's a lot to ask, but we need you to check it out for us."

David could feel adrenaline pumping through his body, He hadn't been on a dig in two years. How would he feel about it? If his reaction to what his parents suggested was any barometer, he knew he wouldn't be sending out applications for a teaching position when he returned home. The mere mention of the dig prompted an unexpected excitement within him.

"I'll have to change my reservations and call Chris, but I guess I can check it out for you. Where is this place, actually located?"

David wrote down the directions as his brother dictated them. From the way Brandon spoke, David knew he was tracing them from a map of Kenya.

"How long do you think it will take you to get there?" his father asked.

"By road, about three to four days, but I think I can persuade Jeff to there me there in the helicopter. We'll fly to Nairobi today and be there sometime tomorrow morning."

"Good." Evan's voice sounded relieved. "Don't worry about

calling Chris. We'll call her when we finish talking to you."

"I know this wasn't what you planned to do, but we do appreciate it," his mother said. "I'll start looking into teaching positions for you. As you know there is a shortage of teachers and I'm certain I can find several openings on the Internet that will be a good fit for you. I'll have a list ready for you when you get home."

David nodded, as if this primitive phone was hooked to the vision phone system, he knew his parents usually used. "I'll contact you tomorrow night and let you know what I find. Since they sent you and e-mail, they must have a computer system."

He ended the call, wondering why his family hadn't used an e-mail to contact him. It was probably too iffy. With the preparations to leave the mission, they must have assumed he would have no time to check the computer for a message he wasn't expecting.

Turning from the phone, he saw Jeff standing behind him. I guess I owe you an explanation."

"You don't owe me anything."

"Yes, I do. I've been trying to put my life together and in doing so, I wasn't completely honest with you. I knew with a common name like Clark, no one would question me about my family. I tried to do the same thing my mother did twenty-five years ago. I guess we have to learn from our own mistakes."

"What are you talking about?"

He could barely believe Jeff hadn't guessed his true identity. The one-sided conversation he'd couldn't help but hearing, must have uncovered David's deception. "Do the names Even Clark and Jaycee Grant-Clark mean anything to you?"

Jeff's puzzled expression surprised David. They'd watched the movie together. Hadn't any of it stuck with the man? How could anyone, in this day and age, not recognize the names of his parents? "What about Round Tree Dig?"

A light of recognition flashed in Jeff's eyes. "You're *that* Clark?" What have you been doing here for the past two years?"

"It's a long story. If I can persuade you to take me to a dig called UMBA, I promise, I'll tell you everything."

After their breakfast, David tried to decide how to explain the reasons behind why he'd kept his background a secret from everyone at the mission, He certainly had nothing to hide, nothing to be ashamed of. So, why was he apprehensive?

Still lost in his thoughts, David finished his packing before saying his good-byes. He hated leaving here.

He et his mind wander to the people he'd met and helped. Over the past two weeks, the people in the surrounding villages honored him. They'd even offered the daughter of one of the influential families as a bride. He remembered gracefully declining the offer. It wasn't the first such proposal he'd received.

In another village, the girl's father was ready to set a bride price, when he told them he owned no cattle. These beautiful people still lived by the old ways and could no comprehend a life without the wealth of cattle. It still amazed him how they were able to cling to their ancient ways while the modern world encroached around them.

David crossed the compound, his backpack securely in place. In an attempt to travel light, he'd shipped the majority of his possessions back home the first of last week. It left him with only the contents of his backpack and a small suitcase. Throwing the suitcase and backpack behind the seat, he climbed into the cockpit, next to Jeff.

"Why didn't you tell me about your parents before this?" Jeff questioned, once they were airborne.

"I didn't think you would understand."

"What's there to understand? Unless of course, if you're ashamed of them."

David realized just how foolish his reasons sounded. No matter how foolish they sounded, they were the only reasons he could find. He had no recourse but to give them to Jeff.

"All of my life, everyone knew about my folks. They expected a kit of me, especially in school. When I went away to college, I decided to go where no one knew me. Beloit College, in Wisconsin seemed as far away as I could get. Hearing you talk about Kenya; I knew I wanted to come here. It's given me the time I needed to decide about the future."

The words hung in the air like fog in the morning. David hardly breathed waiting for Jeff to say something, anything.

"What's there to decide?"

"Whether to get my doctorate in Anthropology or teaching history on the high school level."

"Is it presumptuous of me to ask what decision you reached?"

"No. Until I got the call from my parents this morning, I'd decided to look for a teaching position when I got back to the states."

"After you talked to them, did you change your mind?"

"Let's just say, I'm not so sure anymore. My dad used to say he's like an old fire horse. All he has to do is hear, about a new did, a new find, and he wants to explore it. I guess I'm a lot more like him than I ever thought. He only told me a little about UMBA, but I'm excited about seeing it for myself."

"What does UMBA have to do with your dad?"

"Dr. Kaufman sent him an e-mail yesterday. He's convinced, he's found a parallel society to Round Tree, Dad and Brandon want me to authenticate it."

"Can you? Isn't it almost impossible to detect a hoax?"

"It's not as hard as you think. I grew up reading the writings and playing with the artifacts. There are certain things even our advanced technology can't duplicate."

"All I can say is watch out for Kaufman. If he thinks he's found a parallel society, he won't believe you if you don't authenticate it."

David looked at Jeff. He couldn't possibly know the man David would be meeting tomorrow. "Do you know him?" he finally inquired.

"Not really. I met him last year in Nairobi. I went there for a conference on antiquity. That's what they were calling it. They were focusing on the necessity of maintaining the local customs. Kaufman used the conference as a soapbox to get more funding for UMBA. I think the government gave him some sort of a donation as well as permission to operate the dig for ten years."

David made no comment, He knew how important funding was to a dig. "Did he give you any idea what UMBA stands for?" he asked.

"He didn't go into it. He was too wrapped up in what he hoped to find."

"I can understand why. For the past twenty-five years, archaeologists all over the world have been trying to find out where the man gods took the people when they left Round Tree. They're all looking for the same notoriety my dad received. Everyone want to be remembered for something."

"I can vouch for people remembering what your folks found. I was just a kid back then, but I remember the publicity it generated. As for the movie, I didn't pay much attention to it the other night. I saw it so many times when I was growing up, I knew the plot, almost by heart. I was always intrigued by someone hearing voices and realizing they'd actually lived before."

David nodded. Although he accepted his mother's reincarnation as fact, he doubted her perception he carried the spirit of Sayo. He never mentioned it outside of the family. How could he possibly be reincarnated from a long dead priest? Especially one who so cruelly sacrificed prisoners and took the virginity of young women? In reality, it was something too ridiculous to be true.

The Nairobi airport came into view and with it the heliport where Jeff would land and store their craft.

Not far from the airport was the mission house where they would spend the night. The air-conditioned comforts of the house made David feel as if he were back home. In the past two years, he'd visited Nairobi and stayed at the mission house six times. He decided he would surely miss Brian and Joanne Larson, as well as their hospitality. Tonight, was to have been his last visit. He'd spent the last two weeks preparing to say his good-byes. Now he wondered how many more times he would visit before he left Kenya for good.

"It's wonderful to see you again," Joanne greeted them when they entered the house.

David hugged her and shook hands with Brian. *Eventually, I will leave Kenya. When I do, I'll miss coming to this house and being engulfed in its loving family.*

"We'll miss you when you leave for the states tomorrow," Brian assured David.

"David isn't leaving tomorrow, at least not for the state," Brian advised them.

Brian's questioning expression prompted David to repeat the circumstances surrounding his father's phone call earlier in the day. Again, he explained his background, including his credentials for going to UMBA to authenticate Kaufman's find.

"I don't envy you the task you're about to undertake," Brian cautioned. "Conrad Kaufman is not an easy man.'"

Throughout his narrative, David focused his gaze on the rose pattern of the worn carpeting on the living room floor. Brian's statement caused David to meet the older man's eyes. "I take it you know him."

"We met in college, twenty years ago. As I recall, he was as dedicated to anthropology as I was to theology. Your father's find fascinated him. As more and more of the contents of the writings found at the site of Round Tree were released, he insisted a parallel society had to exist somewhere on the planet. I did some studying and thought perhaps such a society did exist in or near the pyramids of Egypt. The Round 'tree writings are quite similar to hieroglyphics, if my perception is correct."

"You are indeed correct. If Sayo had more time to study with Zandar, the man-god who fathered him, I think you would have seen even more similarities."

"The way you talk it's as though you know this Sayo personally," Joanne observed.

David smiled. Joanne certainly didn't know how close she came to the truth. "Maybe I do. Not personally, of course, but I do know him through the writings. I've read through most of the scrolls and feel I have an insight into his character."

"I don't think David is interested in rehashing the issues surrounding Round Tree," Jeff said. "What more can you tell him about Dr. Kaufman?"

"In my father's day," Brian began, "Conrad would have been called a male chauvinist."

"I what?" David asked unfamiliar with the term.

Joanne was quick to answer. "Before the turn of the century, in the seventies and eighties, I think, women started to come into their own. They called their movement Women's Lib. There were several men, so I'm told, who didn't approve. They thought women should stay at home and have babies. The thought of them entering the workplace intimidated the poor souls."

"So," David questioned, puzzled by Joanne's statement, "what does this have to do with Kaufman?"

The man has such little respect for women, he won't even allow a female to volunteer for his projects," Brian answered. "He also works very hard to inflict his opinions on everyone around him. It's very annoying."

David laughed. "He sounds a bit egotistical, if you ask me."

"It's not just women he pouts down. It's young people in general," Joanne continued. "I'm afraid you won't receive a warm welcome from him."

"I agree," Brian added. "If you declare his find a hoax, he won't believe you. If, on the other hand, you authenticate it, he'll order you to leave. He won't tolerate you stealing his recognition or as my father would have said, his thunder."

"If that's the case, he will have to get over it. If he has found another Round Tree, I'll be staying. The only people on this earth who know more about this project that I do are my parents and my brother, Brandon. No matter what Kaufman wants, they can't get away from Round Tree right now. I'm going to UMBA as their representative. One way or another, he'll have to accept it."

Lying on one of the twin beds in the Larson's guest bedroom, David thought about what Brian said concerning Kaufman. It would be easy to reinstate his reservations to London for tomorrow. It would be just as easy to send an e-mail to his dad insisting either he or Brandon should be the one who would meet with Kaufman.

Easy, yes, but not practical. I'm the one who is in Kenya. I'm the one who can be there tomorrow. Even without my doctorate, I'm the one who can authenticate Kaufman's find. Like it or not, he'll have to deal with me.

Awake in a New World
The New World Book One

Caroline Lewis feels life isn't worth living when she loses her husband to Covid-19 while on a business trip to China. In order to avoid the coming pandemic, she opts to have her body frozen to be awakened in 2070. In 2120, archaeologists exploring the ruins of Los Angeles find Caroline's perfectly preserved body. As she is brought to life, fifty years later than expected, she is forced to learn to live in a world unlike the one she remembers from 2020. Aaron Phillips knows Caroline is special when he hires her as a research volunteer at the library. He hopes she feels the same way about him.

Unwanted in a New World
The New World Book Two

Orphaned at birth, Christopher is sent to a ranch for unwanted children. When he ages out, he is embraced by a militant group of skinheads who are unaware of his Native American heritage. A protest at an Alien Complex outside of Denver opens a new path for his life. While he is receiving his education, his new friends and mentors are working behind the scene to find his birth family.

Melian has come to the complex from the Alien base under the Antarctic ice cap. She takes an immediate interest in Christopher, who now wants to be called Chris, and looks forward to see what their future holds.

Alone in a New World
The New World Book Three

As a child of four, Marco is all alone in the world. With only his mother in his life, her death prompts the authorities to send him to Henderson Ranch for boys. At the age of eighteen, he is sold into slavery to a ranch in Mexico. Two years later, he is recued and reunited with his childhood friend, Christopher. At his friend's insistence he modernizes his name to Mark and embarks on a journey that will bring him full circle back to Henderson Ranch, now called Resurrection Ranch. On his journey, Mark finds previously unknown family and love with one of the alien nurses, Kara, all of whom are willing to journey with him into the future at Resurrection Ranch.

Lost and Found in a New World
The New World Book Four

Peter was kidnapped by his father and sold to Henderson Ranch. There he worked without an education, until his eighteenth birthday when he was sold as a slave to a ranch in Mexico. Once he was rescued, he reunited with some of the others he'd known at Henderson Ranch as well as the mother he'd never forgotten. Helping his friends, Chris and Mark, he becomes involved in the rebuilding of the ranch where they grew up, renaming it Resurrection Ranch, where others like themselves, can work and be given the education they were deprived as children. Before leaving for the ranch, he meets Jerilyn, a therapist who will be transferring to Resurrection Ranch. Almost instantly, he knows she is someone he wants in his life.

Reserruction in a New World
The New World Book Five

When Mark found not only his paternal grandmother but also his step-mother and half siblings, he is amazed when they decide to relocate to Resurrection Ranch to work with those dedicated to bringing their vision to fruition. Chris and Peter's families are also involved in the rebuilding what they hope could be one of the top ranches and educational facilities in the country. They are aided by several aliens who have come to add their expertise to the project. All is well until someone tries to sabotage everything they have dreamed of and built.

The Return of the Ancients
The Aliens Book One

Nina is devastated when she realizes she must leave Plantas along with the man who is to become her mate, Ragnar, and her best friend, Tarena. When Nina arrives on Earth in Peru at the Nazca plains, she is greeted by a young archaeology student, Rand Jacobson. Even though she is attracted to Rand, she is still grieving the loss of Ragnar.

Ragnar is surprised when, after being greeted as a god on the planet Seros, the military opens fire on his family. After being taken prisoner, he is treated like a lab rat until a scientist, Geni, comes to his rescue. At her estate, he learns the physicians who work with her have saved the lives of his family and friends.

My Uncle the King
The Aliens Book Two

When three contingencies took off from their dying planet, Plantas, only two arrived at their destination unharmed. When the lost contingency is hit with a meteor storm, only one ship survives and makes it to their destination of Nalo. Over the generations, the descendants of the original refugees become the ruling class of their adopted planet. Even the rebel group, the Pure Of Nalo, are unable to unseat the monarchy. When relations with Earth are established, it is Prince Nicos who leaves Nalo to find love on an alien planet and bring back new ideas as well as his Earthly family to save the throne and the people of Nalo.

You Again

While attending college at the University of Wisconsin in the 1960s, Carole Martinson fell in love and eloped with Phillip Vanderlin. When his parents realized she was a farmer's daughter and below them socially, they insisted they divorce.

Fast forward to 2019 and Carole is invited to a wedding cruise financed by her granddaughter's fiancé's grandfather. With no knowledge about the groom's family, Carole flies to Florida for the cruise she and her second husband never got to take. Upon her arrival, she immediately recognizes Phillip.

Phillip never forgot his first love. He is thrilled when he realizes the grandmother is the girl he was forced to leave behind so many years ago.

About the Author

Sherry Derr-Wille began her writing career in her sophomore English class in high school. Challenged to get an A on the first test, she won the right to sit in the back of the room and write for a year. At the end of the year no one told her to stop the assignment, so she didn't. At her 40th class reunion, she realized she was the only one who enjoyed the assignment. It was too late because by that time she'd signed seventeen contracts for her work.

Wife to her high school sweetheart of over fifty years, she is the mother of three, grandmother of nine and great-grandmother of six. She is retired and lives in a mid-sized town close to the Illinois border in Southern Wisconsin. Her mantra is READ LOCAL AND BE TRANSPORTED TO ANOTHER WORLD.

www.ingramcontent.com/pod-product-compliance
Lightning Source LLC
Chambersburg PA
CBHW070323130626
46556CB00007B/2712